Gary took a sm...

"There's so much [...] don't hurry up and [...] my chance. Chloe, I know I haven't always done or said the right thing. But do you think you could ever trust me again?"

Chloe shifted uncomfortably, averting her gaze from his steady one. She clasped her hands tightly in front of her. "Trust? I think that's a little difficult for both of us, don't you agree? It's the source of all our problems. I wish. . ." She faltered, unsure how to continue under Gary's watchful eyes.

"You wish what?" he pressed.

"I wish I knew how everything would work out. I wish I had known before." She couldn't help the rush of tears that came to her eyes. Embarrassment made her look away so Gary wouldn't see how vulnerable she was.

The wind was picking up speed, making the waves choppier. The boat rocked heavily. Chloe swayed. Balancing on the deck suddenly took all her attention. Gary gripped her arm and held her gently.

"The storm is coming." He didn't seem concerned.

Chloe wished she felt so calm. Her stomach churned as the boat rocked and lurched on the waves. The combination of the storm and Gary's touch made her uneasy. "You don't seem worried," she whispered.

Gary shrugged. "There's nothing to worry about—unless you get seasick easily. Then we may have a problem." He took a step closer to Chloe. "Do you really think it was a mistake?"

Chloe knew he was referring to the kiss. Color crept into her cheeks. "I'm not sure. I know I didn't handle it well when you wanted to talk about it. I just didn't want to discuss it in front of Brent."

Gary nodded. "And that was my mistake. I never should have brought it up without making sure no one else was around. Can we start over—again?" He took another step toward her. "We could give it another try and find out if. . ."

"If it was a mistake?" she asked, only to fill the charged silence.

TISH DAVIS lives in Florida with her husband and three sons. When she isn't home schooling, she is busy writing inspirational romance. *To the Extreme* was her first published novel. Tish hopes her writing will entertain, uplift, and draw her readers into a closer relationship with the Lord.

Books by Tish Davis

HEARTSONG PRESENTS
HP426—To the Extreme
HP477—Extreme Grace
HP557—If You Please

Real Treasure

Tish Davis

Heartsong Presents

Dedicated to my husband and best friend, Bradley. I love you!

A note from the author:
I love to hear from my readers! You may correspond with me by writing:

Tish Davis
Author Relations
PO Box 719
Uhrichsville, OH 44683

ISBN 1-59310-497-9

REAL TREASURE

All of the characters and events in this book are fictitious. Any resemblance to actual persons, living or dead, or to actual events is purely coincidental.

All scripture quotations, unless otherwise indicated, are taken from the HOLY BIBLE, NEW INTERNATIONAL VERSION®. NIV®. Copyright © 1973, 1978, 1984 by International Bible Society. Used by permission of Zondervan Publishing House. All rights reserved.

PRINTED IN THE U.S.A.

prologue

Chloe's heart beat faster when she saw Gary's car pull up at the curb. He was the most handsome man she'd ever known, and she loved him with all her heart. It didn't matter to her that her father didn't like him. Gary was in college—just a poor student. Having money meant everything to her father. Her mother also had misgivings. She thought the relationship was too serious, too fast for a girl still in high school. She understood her mom's concerns, but that didn't stop her from loving Gary. He was wonderful! He was determined and energetic. He was going to be a famous marine biologist someday, and she would be right there by his side. Together, they would face everything. She knew God approved of the relationship. For years she had prayed for her own prince charming, someone who would cherish her. He couldn't be gruff and insensitive like her father. He had to be adventuresome yet conscientious, strong yet tender. And she had found her prince charming in Gary Erickson.

Sometimes Gary was difficult. He wanted things done his way, and he could be an unrelenting perfectionist. At moments he reminded her of her father, but he was never so harsh. These traits didn't matter to Chloe. Regardless of his faults, she loved Gary unconditionally.

The expression on Gary's face was grim as he approached the door. His blond hair was tousled as though he had repeatedly run his hand through it. He always mussed his hair when he was agitated. His brows were knit in a frown, and the corners of his mouth turned down.

"What is it? What's wrong?" Chloe asked, stepping out to meet him.

"I don't know how to tell you this, so I'll just do it." He pulled away when Chloe touched his arm. The simple action dismayed her. He had never done that before.

"I've met someone else. She's sophisticated. Beautiful. We really clicked. I've never been with anyone so exciting."

Chloe's heart plummeted to her shoes leaving a gaping, painful emptiness. No! This can't be happening! I am supposed to be with Gary forever! "What are you saying?" she whispered, dreading the answer. She knew what he was about to say. She wanted to cover her ears and run for the house. If she didn't hear the words then they didn't exist! She and Gary would stay together. They loved each other with a love that was supposed to last forever! Forget this other woman!

"It's over, Chloe. I'm sorry."

one

Six Years Later

Chloe Crenshaw looked up from the book she was reading. It was one of her favorite books about one of her favorite topics—diving in search of sunken ships. She was fascinated with the ocean and everything it held in its depths. Unfortunately she couldn't concentrate on the book because of the heated discussion that was taking place not far from her. The university study lounge had been a quiet place just a moment earlier.

"What do you mean you're quitting? You can't quit! I forbid you to quit!"

Chloe cringed, recognizing the bellowing voice before she even looked up. It belonged to Professor Gary Erickson. It galled her that he had just started teaching at her university. She hadn't seen him for six years—not since he dumped her for another woman. It took almost all of those years for her to get over him. Imagine the nerve of the guy! Chloe spent countless nights trying to conjure up images of what the woman might look like. It had made her physically sick to think of him embracing someone else, whispering endearments to her. But somehow she had gotten over him. The dull pain was no longer resident in her chest. She didn't think of him every moment of every day. She had actually moved on to another relationship and had gotten engaged—and then broken the engagement. But that didn't matter. She was moving forward with God's capable help. The past was behind her.

And now her safe haven had been encroached. Gary took

a position at her university as the department head of marine biology sciences. It wouldn't have been so bad—the campus was large, and she wouldn't have ever seen him—except that the literature department was next to the biology department. Their classrooms were directly across the hall from each other.

When Chloe first heard the news of his arrival, she couldn't believe it to be true. She thought he would have moved to somewhere in the South Pacific to continue his research long ago. That was a comfortable distance away; teaching across the hall was far too close for her comfort. Her coworkers didn't understand her reticence when it came to Professor Gary Erickson. They all mooned over him, finding him to be the youngest, most handsome instructor in their corner of the campus. Chloe prevented herself from fawning over him only because she never really forgot the pain he'd caused her.

The voices brought Chloe back to the present. She sank lower behind the cover of her book, wishing she could sneak out unobserved.

"I told you I was quitting three weeks ago. My daughter is having a baby soon, and I have to be here for her. I can't be on a boat in the Gulf of Mexico when she needs me. Did you just now figure out that I'm serious?"

Chloe had to admire the short, mousy woman, Mrs. Phipps. Gary was a perfectionist and expected too much of Mrs. Phipps' time and talents. Chloe was surprised it had taken her this long to quit.

"I just found the memo on my desk this morning. So you can surely understand why I'm upset. We leave the day after tomorrow!" His voice rose in agitation with each word.

"Find someone else, Gary. I can't go with you," Mrs. Phipps answered evenly.

Secretly, Chloe cheered Mrs. Phipps for her courage to

stand up to the tyrant. However, she kept her eyes averted, pretending to be absorbed in her book. She didn't want to be involved in any dispute with Gary Erickson. She hoped to never speak to him again. As it grew quiet Chloe glanced up, thinking the room was empty. She found Professor Gary staring at her with a thoughtful expression on his face. Chloe stiffened, uncomfortable under his scrutiny. Lord, don't let him talk to me. Please, don't let him talk to me!

Too late.

"Chloe Crenshaw."

Her name sounded strange on his lips. Chloe suppressed the smirk rising to her lips. It was the first time he had spoken to her in six years. Why did her heart have to betray her by pounding furiously in her chest?

"Nice to see you, Gary," she mumbled. The words sounded insincere. They were insincere. It wasn't nice to see him. Why did he have to show up in her carefully ordered world? She fingered the ends of her hair. It hung straight to her shoulders, and she wished she had taken a little more effort with her appearance that morning. Though she was petite and had a nice figure, she often wore baggy clothes that hid her curves. Today she wore a loose denim skirt with a long oversized shirt. No makeup. No eye appeal.

"What are you doing this summer?" he asked casually, but Chloe knew his curiosity was anything but casual. She stiffened, preparing for possible combat.

"Is that a pickup line?" Chloe's question surprised even herself. She quickly averted her gaze before color flooded her cheeks. Of course it wasn't a pickup line! If he had ever truly been interested in her, he never would have broken up with her in the first place. She turned to face him.

Gary grimaced, his blond hair falling over his forehead. "No," he answered gruffly. "It's actually a plea from a desperate man."

Chloe didn't want to deal with his problems; she had her own. Her ex-fiancé was a problem, along with her father's ever-present temper. She knew he would be furious when he found out her summer class had been canceled along with any hopes of a good paycheck. She turned back to her book and tried to dismiss the man standing across from her. Unfortunately the words seemed to blur on the page. "Find a student to help you. There's always someone looking for a summer adventure."

Gary shoved his hair back from his forehead. "I've already got two students going. What I need is a female chaperone. Someone who can help with the observations and documentation would be a bonus."

Chloe put down her book and studied him curiously. Gary hadn't changed much in six years. He was still lean but more muscular. His thick, sun-bleached blond hair was the same. He needed a haircut, judging by the way his hair kept falling forward over his forehead. His face looked a little older, more experienced. His blue eyes still glimmered with intensity—that would probably never change. She wondered how she stood under his scrutiny. Then she reminded herself that she didn't care what he thought about her.

"What makes you think I'm the right person to chaperone?" she asked, toying self-consciously with her hair.

Gary shrugged. "I'm taking a chance. Like I said, I'm desperate. The pay is lousy, but the sights are great. We're traveling down the Gulf Coast along Mexico to Rancho Nuevo. We'll be following a sea turtle to her nesting beach. The trip will take several weeks. What do you say?"

He hadn't mentioned anything of their history together. It was as if he'd never known her. Fine. She could play the same game and consider his offer as though he were a perfect stranger. Would she want to chaperone on a boat that followed a sea turtle? It was a peculiar notion. Yet it was the best offer Chloe had for the next few months.

Her summer wasn't going according to plan. Two weeks ago she was supposed to get married. Thankfully, Chloe realized before it was too late that she couldn't marry her fiancé, Trevor Renolds. Now, without a summer class to teach, her calendar was open. And she definitely didn't want to hang around home too much. Her father would never tolerate that.

"I'd like a little time to think about it." She didn't believe her request was unreasonable. Passing her summer chasing a turtle was something she needed to consider. She wasn't convinced she could be in the same proximity with Gary. Yet spending time on a boat, touring the Gulf of Mexico, had definite appeal. Not to mention that her father wouldn't be able to grumble at her.

"Time isn't an option," Gary answered impatiently. "I'll call you tonight. I've got to have your answer."

"Fine." Chloe scribbled out her phone number and handed it to him. She doubted he had retained her number from six years earlier.

≈

After her unexpected meeting with Professor Gary, Chloe hurried home. She wanted to discuss the job offer with her mom, Allison Crenshaw. She knew her mom would have some good insight. She found her in the kitchen, making a cheesecake.

"Mm, my favorite!" Chloe said softly, startling her mother.

"Oh, Chloe! I wasn't expecting you so soon," she whispered.

"Is Dad sleeping?" Chloe asked.

"Yes, and he chose the couch again. I don't know why he can't sleep in the bedroom. It would make my life so much easier. I can't get any work done when I have to tiptoe around him."

Chloe didn't have to ask her mom to explain. Her father usually came home in the middle of the day to take a two-hour nap. During the day he sold cars; at night he ran the graveyard shift at the twenty-four-hour supermarket. He was often tired, overworked, and frustrated. Chloe noticed the bottle of antacid on the counter.

"Is his ulcer bothering him again?" she asked.

"Yes, and you know it only gets worse when he's agitated. One of the kids quit at the supermarket, putting extra pressure on your father. He was a bear when he came home this morning. I was glad you'd already left."

Chloe was glad, too. Throughout the years, Chloe had often been her father's scapegoat whenever something was bothering him. While her mom could calm him, Chloe had the opposite effect. Her father could never be considered a nurturing person. He was often angry and found fault with everything Chloe did. Chloe learned early on to avoid her father and not to seek his approval. She'd always wanted him to be pleased with her, but searching for fulfillment always ended in disappointment.

"I have something I want to discuss with you," Chloe said, pulling out a chair at the table. Her mother wiped her hands on a towel and took a seat next to Chloe.

"I've been offered a job for the summer. It's not the best job, but it will get me away for a while."

"Sounds like you've already decided to accept it. What sort of job is it?" her mother asked as she patted her short, dark curls into place.

"I'm going to assist Professor Gary Erickson on one of his marine excursions. I'll be a part of the crew. We leave the day after tomorrow." She held her breath, waiting for her mom's reaction.

Her mom frowned. "Professor Gary Erickson? Do my ears deceive me?"

"It's the same Gary Erickson. I didn't mention this before, but he started teaching at the university a few months ago."

Chloe snatched a ballpoint pen from the table and started fidgeting with it.

She stared at Chloe in concern. "Are you sure it's a wise idea? Is he looking to renew the relationship?"

Chloe thought about Gary's agitation and his need to quickly fill the position. She had been available, and he'd snatched at the opportunity. He would have taken any breathing victim. "There's no possibility of a relationship, Mom. He needs a chaperone, and I need a change of scenery."

Her mom sighed. "Yes, I think you do need a change. After the disappointment two weeks ago, your father certainly has been less than pleasant toward you. He really thought your marriage to Trevor was a good idea. After everything that's happened, I'm sure you feel you need to get away. And now that I think of it, my brother mentioned something about hiring out his boat for the summer. I wonder if it's the same excursion."

"Uncle Howard's boat? Is he going to skipper it?" Chloe's prospects were looking brighter. Her uncle owned a large luxury yacht named The Bounty. He rented it out to wealthy vacationers, took out customers on deep-sea fishing trips, and cruised the coast every chance he got. He was a longtime bachelor with a thick belly, silver top, and more laugh lines in his face than anyone Chloe knew. He was older than his sister by fifteen years. Chloe hadn't spent much time with him over the years. Her father didn't approve of Howard's carefree lifestyle. Despite Uncle Howard's black sheep status with the family, Chloe adored him and couldn't wait to spend time with him. He was the only man she really trusted.

"I'm not sure if Howard will take the tour personally, or if someone else will be hired. I may be mistaken in thinking it's his boat. Anyway, I don't think it was a mistake that your class was canceled. I think God has bigger plans for you. I'm just not sure it will be good for you to be with Gary Erickson. But it would be good for you to get away from anything that will remind you of the disappointment."

Chloe didn't want to think about the "disappointment." Since the wedding fell through two weeks ago her father had been irate. It had cost him big bucks to pay for that wedding and, when it didn't happen, he became unreasonably difficult. She tried to convince him it was for the best. He wouldn't listen. He still believed Trevor Renolds should be her husband.

Chloe knew calling off the wedding had been the right thing to do. Trevor had been growing more and more difficult as the wedding date drew near. He didn't like her plain brown hair; she needed to try the stylist he chose. Her shoes were wrong. Her clothes weren't trendy enough. She spent too much money on books. She needed to go to his church because prominent people attended there. She needed to cover her mouth when she laughed because of her slightly crooked teeth. He went so far as to suggest she try colored contacts to liven up her dull brown eyes. She'd never thought there was anything wrong with her eyes. They reminded her of the color of chocolate. Trevor didn't agree. And the longer she knew him, the less they agreed upon.

What she finally realized was that she didn't love Trevor. She never tried to compare him to Gary, but subconsciously she had. And Trevor never measured up. What made the breakup easier was knowing he didn't love her either—not for herself, anyway. He manipulated her and always made her feel she was second best. She knew she couldn't spend her life with someone like that.

Their breakup wasn't the explosive argument Chloe anticipated. Trevor didn't react when she broke off their engagement. He wasn't angry or upset. He said they would talk about it when she could be reasonable.

Her mother patted Chloe's hand, bringing her thoughts back to the present. "At any rate, you have my blessing to go, as long as you think you can deal with Gary. I'd hate for you to be miserable all summer."

"I think Uncle Howard can handle him. But if he's too difficult, I'll jump ship at the nearest port and fly home."

As Chloe was packing a half hour later the phone rang. She raced to answer it, hoping it hadn't roused her father. Her father hated it when something other than his alarm clock woke him. She picked up the receiver, but she was too late. She could hear her father grumbling in the next room.

"Hello?" she breathed.

"Can I speak with Chloe Crenshaw?" It was Gary. He sounded professional and detached, but that didn't matter to her nerves. Her heart started racing in her chest. Her breathing came out in short, anxious gasps. She forced herself to calm down before she answered.

"This is Chloe."

"Have you made a decision yet?" he demanded.

Chloe glanced at her watch. He'd given her less than two hours to make the decision, but it didn't matter. "Yes, I've decided." There was a loud crash in the family room followed by more of her father's oaths. Chloe cringed.

"And what have you decided?" Gary pressed in agitation.

Before Chloe could answer, her father stomped into the room, glowering at her. "So it's your fault I'm awake!" he bellowed. "I supposed it's one of your little friends calling to gossip. Don't people know I have to work hard? I need sleep! I can't have the phone ringing at all hours of the day. You are so ungrateful, Chloe! Why did God force you upon me?"

Chloe cringed as the line became silent against her ear. She knew Gary had heard every word her father spoke, and she felt mortified.

"I get no appreciation from you. You're so selfish! Can't you find something worthwhile to do while I'm resting?"

"Chloe?" Gary asked after a tense moment while her father continued to rage. Chloe could barely hear Gary's voice.

"Yes?" she whispered.

His voice lost its agitation. "Can I count on you?"

"Yes." She was thankful Gary didn't make any comments about her father's temper. They used to argue over her father's behavior, the way he yelled at her and blamed her for everything.

"Show up at the pier at six thirty on Thursday morning. We're in slip number thirty-eight. The boat's name is The Bounty."

Chloe's heart leapt with gladness. It was her uncle's boat! "I'll be there," Chloe whispered before she hung up. Thursday couldn't come soon enough.

Chloe turned to her glaring father. He was finished ranting, and now the guilt-trip would begin. Chloe tried to head it off by explaining the phone call. "That was one of the professors from the university," she explained stiffly. Her father never liked Gary, so she omitted the fact that he was the professor she had spoken with.

Her words had no effect on her father. "The sooner you move out the better," he grumbled. "When are you going to do that? You can't continue to put such a burden on me and your mother. You should have married when you had the chance. Who will marry you now?"

Chloe resisted the urge to argue with her father. At one time his words hurt her, and perhaps they still did if she acknowledged the truth. But more than anything, his attitude irritated her. She knew she wasn't a burden on the household. Her teaching paychecks from the university covered the utilities and grocery bills. She wasn't sure why her father blamed her for the troubles in his life.

She knew deep down that her father really did care for her, in a rather undeveloped way. Her mother had always made sure that Chloe didn't connect her father's method of parenting with the way her Heavenly Father viewed her. It would be easy to believe all fathers were harsh and annoyed. Yet she had seen other fathers who were different than her own. When she was a child her friends' dads seemed so different. They were gentle and attentive. It was confusing to her. Then her mother explained that God would have all fathers adore their children as He adored His creation. But some fathers were so bogged down with the cares of the world that they missed the real treasure. Men, Chloe thought with a sigh. She was beginning to doubt she would find anyone who could appreciate the important things. Her ex-fiancé certainly didn't care for what she felt was important.

In the beginning, Chloe had found Trevor to be charming. His perfectionism hadn't concerned her at the time. Everything he did was in perfect order from the way he dressed to how he planned their dates. He even told Chloe which clothes to wear on their dates so they would complement each other. His attention to detail was endearing. She liked how he sent roses to her house every Friday morning. He always ordered for her at restaurants because she took too long deciding for herself. As they continued seeing each other, Trevor insisted on his way more and more. Whenever Chloe tried to disagree with him, he would become very tense and frustrated with her. Chloe began to see that Trevor wanted to control her, and it didn't seem endearing any longer. The longer they dated, the more manipulative he became—and angry. Chloe could see the same anger in both her father and in Trevor. Trevor was able to mask his anger better than her father, but for how long would he choose to hide it?

In her heart, Chloe knew Trevor wasn't the man for her. He claimed to trust God just as her father did, but his actions didn't demonstrate godly love. Breaking their engagement had been difficult. It was the first time she had stood against Trevor. She had become such a doormat for him. But God gave her strength, and she was able to hand Trevor's ring back to him.

She hadn't once regretted her decision, even though her father tried to make her change her mind. He thought she was foolish to turn down such a fine man. Most important in her father's eyes was that he made a healthy salary. Despite her father's objections, Chloe knew she had made the right decision, and her mother agreed with her wholeheartedly.

"I'm leaving for several weeks," Chloe said firmly, turning her attention back to her father. He still stood in the doorway of her bedroom, glowering at her.

Her words made him pause. "That long? Where are you going?"

Chloe knew any explanation she might give wouldn't satisfy him. "I've been asked to work on an ocean expedition studying sea turtles."

Gregory Crenshaw snorted. "Studying turtles? What a waste of time! And I suppose taxpayers are carrying the burden. You'd be better off with Trevor. If you had any sense, you would apologize to him for being a fool and marry him. I might be able to salvage some of the expense if you don't wait too long to make up."

Why did her dad have to be such a difficult man? It was all about money! He never once tried to see things from her point of view. He only saw her as a burden, a foolish girl who made his daily life more difficult. She wished he could understand that she wanted a man she could love who would cherish her in return. She didn't want a husband who constantly critiqued how she dressed, the way she cooked, and whether she wore lipstick. She wanted more for her life!

"Dad," Chloe said through clenched teeth, "for the last time, I am not marrying Trevor Renolds! He doesn't love me, and I don't love him. Now please, I need to pack." Her father was gone before she even finished the sentence.

❧

Thursday morning came quickly. The sun was just coming up, and it looked to be another beautiful day. Chloe had been up for two hours. A nervous excitement awoke her, and she hadn't been able to go back to sleep. It was as though she was a child again, waiting to see if Santa had visited her on Christmas morning. The weather was already sticky warm. Chloe wondered what the weather would feel like when they were out to sea. She'd never spent much time on a boat. She'd never even slept on board one. But she could do this; she knew she could.

As Chloe loaded her suitcase into her mother's car, a black sedan pulled to a stop in front of her house. Chloe froze, her breath catching in her throat. "Please, Lord, not him. Not today," she groaned.

The well-dressed, dark-haired man stepped from the car and approached Chloe. She wanted to run into the house and triple lock the door, but she stood her ground, her fists tightly clenched at her sides.

Chloe swallowed hard, forcing words through her stiff lips. "Hello, Trevor."

Trevor stepped closer to Chloe. "You're wearing your hair up."

Chloe self-consciously patted her hair. Her straight tresses were pulled back into a simple ponytail. She knew Trevor didn't approve of her hairstyle. He liked her hair hanging loose around her shoulders.

"Why are you here, Trevor?"

"I stopped by your dad's store last night, and he said you're about to leave on a crazy excursion."

"You saw my father?"

Trevor's brows knit together in annoyance. "That's not the point. I'm here to tell you not to go. I thought we would work out our relationship this summer. I've given you a few weeks to get over your jitters. How can we get back together when you aren't here? You know I'm still willing to marry you despite everything."

Lord, please help me say the right thing to this man. I never express myself well when he's around. My tongue becomes weighted, and I mutter unintelligible words. I won't be his doormat any longer! "I need to hurry, Trevor. Professor Erickson said I must be at the dock at six thirty. I don't want to be late."

"You can be late. I'm sure they'll understand." He flashed her one of his hundred-watt smiles that used to melt her resolve and make her do whatever he wanted. "Besides, I was thinking we could see a movie tonight."

Chloe shook her head. Nothing had changed since they had been apart. Her schedule didn't matter, or what anyone else thought. It was all about Trevor. "No, I can't be late. I need to go now."

Chloe's mom stepped out of the house and paused when she saw Trevor. "It's time for me to take you to the pier, Chloe." Her tone indicated she wasn't pleased to see him.

Trevor held up his hand in a friendly wave. "Hello, Mrs. Crenshaw."

She cast a disapproving look in his direction. "Hello, Trevor. I'm sorry we can't stay to talk, but Chloe has a prior appointment. We shouldn't be late."

"I know about her appointment, and I'm planning to take her." He challenged Chloe with his confident gaze.

Her mom pursed her lips. "I don't know about that." She looked at her daughter. "Chloe?"

Chloe felt the typical powerless feeling sweep over her. It always came when Trevor gave her an ultimatum. There was no alternative but to do what he wanted, just like with her father. Chloe felt as though all her energy had deflated, like a flat, airless balloon. It always seemed easier to agree with him than to constantly fight him. Now she would stand firm against him—but he could have this one concession. "It's all right, Mom," she sighed. "Trevor can take me. Dad will be home from the store soon anyway. He'll need his breakfast."

Chloe wished she had stood up to Trevor. She really didn't want him to take her. The last thing she needed was to have Trevor bombarding her with his questions and opinions in the last minutes before she boarded the boat for several weeks.

"Who is heading up this project?" Trevor asked as he started his car.

Chloe tried not to feel comfortable in the plush leather seat. She held herself stiffly and refused to look at Trevor. "Professor Gary Erickson."

"And have you ever worked with him before? This might not be a positive working relationship. Do you know anything about him? What happens when you find you don't like working with him on board a ship? I'm sure you can't jump off at the nearest island. Have you really thought this through?"

Chloe turned to him, wanting to tell him to keep his questions to himself. When she looked at him the words died in her throat. He was right. She studied Trevor's profile. He certainly pinpointed all of her fears. How did he do that? He had no knowledge of the history between her and Gary. Perhaps Trevor understood her better than she thought. Or maybe he wanted her to feel afraid. He always sought out the worst side of everything, causing fear to rise within her. The fear made her feel helpless and foolish. Yet knowing Trevor as she did, he was only being practical. And in light of all those practical questions, Chloe had to rethink her decision. Could she really spend a summer on a boat with Gary Erickson? She had spent the last six years getting over him. A few weeks with him might renew all the pain she'd worked so hard to release.

Trevor glanced at her in his smug, superior way. He was aware he could manipulate her and make her think differently. Chloe hated his smugness, but she also had to admit that she was about to make a big mistake. Agreeing to work on the excursion had been a hasty decision—a bad decision. No way could she work with Gary Erickson. She sank lower in her seat, feeling terrible.

"Now that you're staying home this summer—"

"How do you know I'm staying home?" The retort was weak.

Trevor reached across the seat and took ahold of Chloe's hand. "I'd really like you to stay. We can rethink our wedding. I understand why you broke off the engagement. Your father explained some things to me. I know you need a firm hand to help steer you in the right direction. He said it isn't right to give you too many choices, because you have difficulty making the right decision. We've seen that, haven't we? This summer trip is just another example of that. Had you asked me first, you never would have gotten yourself into this mess. But I'm here to help you now."

Chloe considered his words. She didn't like Trevor's tone. She wasn't a child needing his direction, yet the situation did feel like a mess. "I don't know," she murmured, growing more confused by the second. If only she clearly knew what God wanted her to do.

"You know how good we are together. I admit I made some

mistakes. I was, perhaps, a little heavy-handed when it came to your appearance. I think it would be fine for you to dress as you please—within reason, of course. I think, also, I had too high of expectations of you. And you have to admit you rarely voiced your own preferences, so it was easy for me to step in. I think we can do better in the future now that we've had time to look at where we went wrong. The second time will be a success."

Chloe had to acknowledge that some of what Trevor said made sense, except the part with her father's advice. She could recognize his words a mile away. You need a firm hand to steer you. You can't handle too many choices. Yet having Trevor admit that he made a few mistakes was something new. Maybe there was a chance they could make it work. She did still care for him, didn't she? Besides, she could use Trevor as an excuse to get out of the excursion. She could tell Gary she couldn't go because she needed to work out personal issues.

Trevor turned his car into the marina parking lot. Sailboats and yachts filled the boat slips. Chloe wondered which one was her uncle's boat, The Bounty. She had only been on the boat once, and that had been several years ago.

"I'll leave the car running while you go tell Professor Erickson why you won't work for him this summer. Hurry back. Then we can go out for breakfast before I have to get to work." Trevor leaned across Chloe and pushed the door open for her.

Chloe didn't argue with him as she slipped from the car. The warm, salty breeze greeted her, and Chloe inhaled deeply. She didn't want to tell Gary that she couldn't join the crew for the expedition. She wasn't sure what she was going to say. After witnessing his outburst when Mrs. Phipps quit, Chloe knew she was in for his wrath. Maybe she could talk to Uncle

Howard instead and have him explain the awkward situation. He used to say he would do anything to see her smile. Perhaps he would bail her out of this situation.

As Chloe approached slip thirty-eight her steps became increasingly slower. A horrible dread filled her chest, making it difficult for her to breathe. I don't want to talk to Gary. He'll be angry and disappointed with me. I'm going to make things so difficult for him, and he'll dislike me even more. I shouldn't have agreed to come in the first place. I don't join last-minute sea voyages with old boyfriends. It's not like me. Trevor is right. I was foolish to even consider this. Lord, help me!

The Bounty was a bigger boat than Chloe remembered. In her mind she thought it was similar to the S.S. Minnow with the Skipper, Gilligan, and Mary Ann. But in reality it was a modern, well-outfitted yacht. Chloe guessed it to be over seventy feet long; its blackened windows contrasted with the all-white exterior.

As Chloe mustered her courage to step aboard, Gary bounded down the gangplank toward her. He was dressed casually in sandals, jean shorts, and a blue flowered shirt. He looked good—and far more relaxed than the last time Chloe saw him. She hoped his casual appearance was a reflection of a relaxed state of mind. Her news might be received better than she expected.

"Good morning, Chloe. Traveling light?" Gary greeted. He actually seemed pleased to see her. The smile didn't slip from his face as he stepped closer to her.

All the things Chloe meant to say flew from her thoughts. Her tongue was left helpless to explain her empty hands. She had to get this over with.

"You aren't planning to bail on me, are you?" His tone was light.

Chloe stared at him, unable to speak.

"Chloe? You aren't ditching me." Now there was a distinct edge to his words.

"I think I made a mistake." Her voice came out hoarse and much weaker than she intended. If only Trevor were there to help her explain. He had convinced her to leave the expedition during the ten-minute ride to the marina; he could give Professor Gary Erickson all the reasons why Chloe needed to remain home during the summer.

"You aren't quitting," Gary countered. He planted his fists on his hips, his gaze challenging her to disagree. His easy smile was gone, replaced by the glower he wore so often. He was formidable when he scowled. It was no wonder he always had Mrs. Phipps scurrying about like a mouse.

"I'm really not up to this," Chloe faltered.

"Where is this coming from? Your father? Or is it because of me?"

Chloe shook her head. "No—I mean—I don't know! I just hadn't thought it through. I don't think this is a good idea." Her hands started shaking, so she clasped them behind her. She felt like a tardy schoolgirl facing the headmaster.

Gary stared at her stubbornly. "Whether you thought it through or not is irrelevant. You made a commitment. I'm counting on you to do your part. Now where is your stuff? We're leaving in half an hour, with or without your belongings."

"But—"

"No buts! You're going. You promised, and I need you." His tone softened. "It won't be as bad as you think."

Chloe knew in her heart that Gary was right. She'd told him he could count on her, and now she was backing out. It didn't matter that they had once loved each other and were now strangers. She always tried to be a reliable person, and here she was telling Gary that he couldn't rely on her. Yet the points Trevor had brought up had been true as well. He knew her weaknesses and how to bend her and change her thinking. She felt torn between the two choices. She could stay home and explore a renewed relationship with Trevor. That was the practical thing to do. He said he'd made mistakes in the past; it was something they could begin with. Or she could go on this wild sea adventure—with a man she had hoped to never see again.

If she was completely honest with herself, she wanted to go on the trip. Her mother was right. Chloe needed to get away from everything and have a fresh start. When she was around Trevor, she didn't think for herself. She needed a chance to be herself without the disapproving glowers of Trevor and her father. Neither would be happy with this decision, and Trevor would be furious, but she needed to go. She wanted to travel, learn about sea turtles, and spend time on her uncle's boat. Gary was also right. She couldn't quit before she even started—even if she had to spend the time with him.

"My suitcase is in the trunk. Over there," she pointed toward the parking lot where Trevor was waiting for her.

"I'll help you with the suitcase. Can't have you jumping in the car and driving off." Gary strode toward the parking lot at a fast clip. Chloe had to jog to keep up with him.

This mess was about to take another interesting turn. Her two exes were about to meet. It felt like a Hollywood plot. And worse than having them meet was telling Trevor she was leaving. It would be no simple task.

"I'm not going to leave now, Gary. You were right. I told you that you could count on me."

Gary's grunt of disbelief made Chloe frown, but she didn't pursue the argument. She pointed to Trevor's car. As they approached, Trevor opened the door and stepped out. He looked like a towering giant, but Gary didn't seem to notice.

"What's going on here?" Trevor demanded.

Chloe shrank back at his angry tone.

"I'm helping to collect Chloe's things. We'll be shoving off soon." Gary tapped on the trunk as though he expected Trevor to open it for him.

Trevor crossed his arms over his chest. "Get in the car, Chloe. I told you that you aren't going."

Gary moved to stand in front of Chloe, blocking Trevor's view of her. "Are you her guardian?"

"No! I'm her fiancé!" Trevor blustered.

"Ex-fiancé," Chloe quipped. She peered around Gary then cowered at Trevor's menacing glare.

Gary squared his shoulders. "Well, pal, she's agreed to work for the expedition this summer, and we're counting on her. She'll send you a postcard. Now, do I have to force your trunk open, or are you going to help us out?"

"Chloe?" Trevor asked, glaring at her.

Chloe shrugged helplessly. "He's right. I gave my word."

"And what about our wedding?"

"It was called off. Remember, Trevor?" Chloe answered softly.

Trevor stiffened then went to the trunk and unlocked it. He hefted out Chloe's suitcase, dumping it on the ground. He slammed the trunk, and without a backward glance he got in the car and sped away.

Chloe guarded herself, expecting Gary to comment on Trevor's behavior, but he said nothing. Instead he jerked up the handle on Chloe's suitcase and started wheeling it toward her uncle's boat, The Bounty.

two

The Bounty wasn't the average college observation vessel. It truly was a luxury yacht. They boarded at the rear of the boat and walked across the aft deck. There was a short, curved stairway to a swim platform. Chloe also saw an undersized counter with a sink in it. There were a tiny refrigerator, a barbecue grill, and a large, round table with six chairs—all on the back deck! Gary didn't give her time to tarry outdoors as he led her through a sliding glass doorway into the main salon.

The salon wasn't what Chloe expected to find on a boat. It was a long, narrow room, about eighteen feet wide. There were a brown leather sofa and two leather recliners. A built-in entertainment center sat between the recliners, and it was loaded with updated media equipment. An antique coffee table sat in front of the sofa. Near the galley was a formal dining area with seating for six. Chloe couldn't see into the galley, but it appeared to be the same size of kitchen found in an apartment.

"Beyond the galley is the pilothouse where the course is plotted and the captain will sometimes steer the boat. Jennifer McRay is your responsibility for this trip. Your stateroom is next to hers on the lower level. That's Jennifer over there." Gary pointed toward a smiling young redhead who'd just stepped through the sliding door into the galley.

Chloe recognized the student from one of the classes she taught at the university. Jennifer was a bright girl with a pleasant disposition. Chloe knew the least of her worries would come from Jennifer. She wondered who else was on the boat.

"I was wondering who skippers this boat. Is Howard—"

"Stow your stuff then come back up to the salon. We'll be leaving in a few minutes," Gary said curtly.

Chloe wanted to ask Gary some questions about the trip and the turtle they were following. But he had already turned away from her to go back out to the aft deck. She knew Gary was angry with her. It was easy to pick up on his body language. Six years seemed to vanish as she watched him walk away, his jaw set, his posture stiff. She wanted to start this adventure on the right foot, yet it seemed the best she could do was stumble. As usual, she had another man angry with her. At least her father wasn't there to criticize her. She was sure he was ranting at her mother right now for letting Chloe go on this "foolish adventure."

Then there was Trevor. It was her father's fault Trevor showed up just before she was to leave. And to think she almost gave in to what he wished! Thankfully Gary had held her to her word. What a mess she would be in at that moment without him! Trevor would probably be setting a new wedding date.

Yet it didn't make her feel any better that her current employer was frustrated and found her unreliable. She would have to work extra hard to prove herself. Now, if only he'd told her where on the boat she was supposed to stow her stuff. If she could find Uncle Howard, he would help her out.

"Um, Jennifer?" Chloe asked as she approached the girl. Jennifer was taking fresh fruit from a crate and putting it into the refrigerator. Chloe noticed there was an ice maker in the door. She also noticed a dishwasher, trash compactor, granite countertops, and a built-in microwave. This boat was incredible!

"Oh, hello, Miss Crenshaw! I'm so glad you came. When I heard that Mrs. Phipps quit at the last minute, I was happy to hear you agreed to chaperone. I hope you brought plenty of sunscreen. If not, I have enough to share. This fair skin is such a hindrance!" Jennifer was a typical redhead in the sense that her skin was pale to the point of being white. Jennifer would probably burn easily. Chloe was thankful that although her nose and cheeks were covered with freckles, at least she tanned quickly.

"Jennifer, since we're going to be shipmates on this voyage, I'd like you to call me Chloe. And while I'm distracting you from your duties, do you think you could show me where to put my stuff?"

"Oh, sure!" Jennifer shut the refrigerator and pointed Chloe toward the stairs that led to the staterooms below. "Isn't this a great boat? I still can't believe we got it for the excursion. I feel like a diplomat or something!"

They went down the stairs, and Jennifer opened a door immediately to the right. "You and I each get our own stateroom. This is yours." Chloe stepped over the threshold and into a small bedroom. A queen-size bed filled the room. It was covered with a silver and black comforter with matching pillows. Under the bed was a built-in dresser. A TV and VCR were built into the wall. Chloe doubted she would watch much television on this trip.

"Over there is your closet or locker," Jennifer said, pointing to a door. "And through that other door is your bathroom. It's called a head on a boat. Nice room, huh? The one next door is Professor Gary's and Brent's. They have bunk beds. I think we got the better end of the deal."

Chloe only half listened to Jennifer chatter as she explored her new room. The bathroom was small with a tiny shower. There was hardly enough room to turn around, but everything was tastefully decorated to match the stateroom.

"Remember to keep your closet door latched. Otherwise

your clothes will go flying all over the room when we hit rough seas."

Chloe tuned in to Jennifer's words. "Does that happen often?" she asked nervously. She hadn't thought about storms at sea. She didn't swim well enough to save herself if the boat sank!

"Severe storms don't come along that often, so don't worry. And we usually have enough warning to avoid dangerous situations. The occasional squall isn't anything to worry about." The girl grinned at Chloe.

Chloe returned Jennifer's smile without enthusiasm. What had she gotten into? She never thought she might be lost at sea in a hurricane. She'd watched the Titanic documentaries. If that glamorous boat could sink, so could this one!

The engines started suddenly, cutting off any questions Chloe might have asked Jennifer. "Looks like we're about to set off!" Jennifer said with a grin of excitement. She darted out of the room with Chloe close at her heels.

Up on the foredeck Chloe found Gary rolling rope. She was surprised to see him doing manual labor instead of setting up his tracking equipment or studying turtle guides. He easily coiled the rope into a tight pile on the deck.

Gary glanced up at her. "Lend a hand, Chloe. I'm going to untie, and I need you to pull in the rope and coil it like this." Before she could ask any questions, he jogged down the gangplank and began untying the heavy ropes.

Chloe pulled in the heavy, wet rope and slowly rolled it like Gary showed her. Her finished product somewhat resembled his, so she hoped he would be satisfied. She wished she could find Uncle Howard. Then maybe she might feel a little more connected on this trip. So far she felt like a fish out of water, and she wasn't sure she could adapt quickly enough to please Gary.

"Thank You, Lord, for making me a quick learner. Help me to not make too many mistakes," she muttered as she wound the second rope and then the third. By the time she was finished her arms felt weak from the effort, and she realized what terrible physical condition she was in. She had a feeling all that would change by the end of the summer.

Gary boarded, securing the gangplank. He gave a thumbs-up to the pilot—presumably her uncle. Chloe felt a shifting of the engines as the boat began pulling away from the dock. She stumbled slightly but regained her footing. Thankfully Gary had his back to her and didn't witness her lack of sea legs. Chloe walked carefully over to the rail and watched their slow progression out of the marina and into the bay. The breeze was warm and more forceful as they moved toward open waters. Chloe was comforted by the gentle dip and rise of the boat over the waves.

"Ever spend much time on a boat?" Gary asked, only inches behind her.

Chloe started, not realizing anyone was near her. "I—um—no." She couldn't get her lips to function properly. Otherwise she would have told Gary that this boat belonged to her uncle.

"You'll get used to it. We won't ever be too far from land because Daisy feeds close to shore."

"Daisy?"

Gary nodded. "The Kemp's ridley turtle we're tracking. Do you know anything about this species?"

Chloe shook her head. "Only that they're green."

Gary wasn't amused. "They aren't really green. They're grayish olive on the carapace. That's the top shell. And a cream color on the underside, which is the plastron. There are eight types of sea turtles, and some of them look green. Ours, the Kemp's ridley, is the smallest and most endangered. They were named after Richard M. Kemp—a fisherman who played at natural history. We're expecting Daisy to nest at Rancho Nuevo along with hundreds of other Kemp's ridleys. It's the primary nesting beach for this species. If she does nest, we'll take some of her eggs back to Texas with us."

Chloe leaned back against the rail, absorbing all the facts he rattled off. "How do you track her? Does she have a homing device or something?" she asked, forgetting about any tension or history between them. She was genuinely interested in sea life, and the mysterious turtles fascinated her.

"Sort of. We attached a remote tracking device to her shell just behind her head. Every time she surfaces for air a signal goes up to our satellite. We then follow her movements through the computer. I've just about got everything set up."

"You said she'll feed close to shore. What does she eat?"

"Mostly crustaceans—crabs are a favorite. She'll eat jellyfish, mollusks, and seaweed. You'll learn a lot about Kemp's ridleys from my notes. I've got a laptop for you to transcribe all my notes. I do mostly dictation into a mini recorder, and you'll use that to copy and organize my notes. I'm terrible with getting my thoughts in order; you'll see. Mrs. Phipps always grumbles at me. If you'd like, I can show you the tracking equipment."

"Transcribing? I thought I was supposed to be a chaperone. You never mentioned any dictation or organizing notes."

Gary frowned. "I didn't? Mrs. Phipps always helps me out. I just assumed. . ." He trailed off.

Chloe could sense his growing agitation. He had made a vague comment about documentation, now that she thought about it. She should have been paying closer attention. In all fairness, she was willing to help. "I'll help you with your notes. Just don't expect me to be as good as Mrs. Phipps."

Gary's demeanor changed instantly from agitated to cheerful. "I'd really appreciate anything you could do." He reached out and squeezed Chloe's hand; the contact surprised her.

Gary's gratitude was also a surprise to Chloe. Her memories of him didn't contain gratitude. She often thought of him as a tyrant, lording power over others as her father and Trevor did. Yet the Gary in front of her didn't seem tyrannical—perhaps a little temperamental. When he gave her a boyish grin Chloe returned a guarded smile. She felt drawn to him, and she knew that was dangerous. No matter how attractive or friendly he seemed, it wasn't smart to trust him. She couldn't make that mistake again. She had to maintain a professional distance and remember he was her colleague—nothing more. Somehow God would help her keep everything in perspective. She was there to do a job.

"Since I'll be working with the equipment, it's probably a good idea that I become familiar with it as soon as possible. Will you show me the computer?" Chloe tried to follow Professor Gary across the deck, but the pitch and roll of the waves caught her off balance. Her small gasp caught Gary's attention, and he shot out his hand to steady her. His fingers were warm on her upper arm, and he held her longer than necessary as she regained her footing.

"By the end of the excursion you'll be a seasoned sailor," Gary promised.

Chloe blushed at the contact and stepped away. "Thanks," she mumbled self-consciously. "I'm sure you're right."

She followed him inside the air-conditioned salon, careful to keep plenty of distance between them. Gary led her to the formal dining table where he had a computer set up. It wasn't fancy and Chloe felt a flicker of disappointment. She was expecting space-age equipment, not a regular desktop computer. The work area resembled a college lab more than a scientific tracking hub.

A sprawling screen saver rolled across the monitor reading,

"God is good. God is faithful." Chloe was reminded of how they used to go to church together, hold hands during worship, and read from the same Bible. He had bolstered her trust in men and encouraged her with his simple faith. She thought they would get married in his little church and have their children dedicated there as well. It seemed decades ago.

Chloe forced her attention back to Gary and what he wanted to show her on the computer. She didn't want to remember the past. It resurrected longings for a husband and children. She wanted to be loved. She wanted to have an adoring husband who came home to her day after day, year after year. And it made her uncomfortable when Gary's face filled the image.

Gary had moved on to another topic and was focusing on the tracking system. "We just use a regular PC that's linked up to the satellite. We also have remote Internet access. Take a look at that." He pulled up the software that showed the coordinates of Daisy's movements. "See her decisive movement down along the coast? I've been watching her movements for two years—long before I came to the university as a professor. I worked with a small group that tagged and studied Daisy and other turtles like her. This is the first year Daisy has taken such a direct line south. My colleagues and I feel this is the year she will nest. You'll be responsible for coordinating all the information."

"And you think I'll be able to accomplish this? I'm not so sure," Chloe said. Some of her earlier anxiety tried to creep back. She knew by the way Gary explained things that he expected a certain standard. She was only a literature teacher. What did she know about the nesting habits of sea turtles?

"You aren't trying to back out again, are you? Have some courage!" His voice was unyielding.

Chloe stiffened. What did he know of her courage? He

hadn't been there when she was picking up the pieces of her heart. Was he joking? He didn't sound like it. He sounded like he was looking for an argument. "Are you ridiculing me? I'm not a child." She shifted in discomfort.

Gary scowled. "I wasn't ridiculing you. Please don't be so sensitive—"

"Please don't pick on me!" she retorted.

"I wasn't picking on you! I was merely making you understand that you can't quit this trip without a really good reason. I need your help."

"I never said I was going to quit. I was just sharing the fact that I may not be perfect enough to fill Mrs. Phipps' shoes!" Chloe felt a hot, angry flush creep up her neck and into her cheeks.

Gary took a deep breath. "Perhaps we could continue this later."

Chloe thought that was a good idea. For whatever reason, they had turned a few silly remarks into an all-out dispute. Part of her wanted to apologize for the argument. No matter how he riled her, she shouldn't have fallen for the bait. Yet he was just as much at fault. "I think I'd like to find my uncle," she murmured.

Gary didn't respond. His back was to her, and his attention was focused on the computer screen.

Chloe quickly crossed the salon to the doors that led to the pilothouse. She was relieved to find her uncle at the helm when she stepped into the room.

"Uncle Howard!"

The man turned, staring at her in surprise. He was in his early sixties, stood over six feet tall, and weighed around 250 pounds. His skin was dark and leathery, no doubt from years in the sun and wind. He hid his silver hair under a ball cap. "Chloe-girl! I can't believe my eyes!" he exclaimed, his blue eyes twinkling with merriment. "What are you doing on my boat, and why didn't I know about it?"

Chloe shrugged sheepishly as she sat on the sofa behind the helm. "It was as much of a surprise to me. Two days ago Professor Erickson asked me to replace someone else on this trip. It came at a convenient time. . . ." She trailed off, thinking of her failed engagement and how angry her father still was with her. "It was a good time for a change of scenery," she finished.

"You don't have to explain to me. I talk to your mother often. My little sister doesn't keep much from me. Obviously Trevor wasn't the right man for you, and I'm glad you saw that before you married him. He would have ruined your life—no matter what your father says. I'm just a little surprised to see both you and Gary Erickson on the same boat together." Howard turned back to the helm's dozens of gauges, switches, and buttons.

There were a GPS navigator, a compass, speedometer, and a small TV screen that displayed the aft deck. Chloe peered closely at the screen. She could see Jennifer sitting on the rear deck, talking with a tall, skinny young man. Chloe assumed he was the other student on the excursion.

"I didn't realize you and Mom shared so much," Chloe murmured.

Mom rarely talked about her brother since Chloe's dad didn't approve of Uncle Howard. He thought Howard was reckless and irresponsible because he chose to spend his life on a luxury yacht. Uncle Howard didn't have a wife or a child, claiming the sea was enough. Chloe found his life exciting. She respected that he'd never married. And after her trouble with first Gary then Trevor, she believed her uncle understood more about relationships than her father gave him credit for. Her dad saw Uncle Howard as a man who couldn't make a commitment. Chloe saw him as a man who didn't have to deal with manipulation and heartbreak.

"How is your mom? I wanted to talk to her before we left, but I didn't get the chance. I'll probably call her when we reach the next port."

"She's fine. She's been thinking about applying for a job at the new flower store, but I doubt that Dad will let her."

Howard frowned. "I've never understood your father. He controls your family with an iron fist."

Chloe sighed, thinking about how angry her father became over small incidents. "I know. And it seems like he gets more frustrated as he grows older. Mom can handle him, though."

"We need to pray for him, Chloe. In the meantime, you need to find a man that will honor you from the very beginning. Then you don't have to pray that God will change him."

"I think it's easier to stay single than to find the right person. I don't want to live with a person like my father, and I almost made that mistake. I won't do it again." Her words came out stronger than she intended, and Uncle Howard studied her. His expression was gentle.

"You can't let one bad experience turn you away from all men. Trust God, Chloe. He won't steer you wrong."

Only one bad experience? She considered her involvement with Gary to be a bad experience. There was a lifetime of walking on eggshells around her father. Then Trevor tried to turn her into a completely different person. She had dozens of experiences telling her to stay single. Men weren't worth the heartache.

"There are a lot more switches and gauges than I expected," Chloe commented, trying to divert his attention away from her. "Do you ever get tired of playing on your boat?"

Howard laughed. "That sounds like your father talking! I chose my lifestyle, and I don't care what he thinks of me. No,

Chloe, I don't ever get tired of it. I meet all sorts of interesting people. Brainy types—like your professor—the rich and famous, middle-class fishermen on vacation. . . I love it. I get to travel to tropical places, spend all my time on the ocean, and get paid well for it. It isn't 'playing on my boat.' It's the best way for me to live."

"I'm sorry, Uncle Howard. I didn't mean to sound disrespectful. You have an incredible boat. I didn't realize it was so luxurious."

Howard shrugged. "It's home. I'm just glad it worked out to take your professor down the coast. I was going anyway to pick up a client in Tampico, Mexico. That's why I agreed to the university's terms. Made the trip south a little more profitable. And as a bonus, I get my niece on board."

Chloe stood, brushing the wrinkles from her shorts. "I hope we'll get enough time to talk on this trip. That professor has a lot of expectations. But I'll try to make time." She stepped to the starboard sliding door and paused when Howard spoke her name.

"Chloe. . ." He paused, as though searching for the right words. "Don't worry so much about men. They aren't all like your dad. Look at me; I'm nothing like him!"

Chloe grinned. No, the deeply tanned man in a striped tank top and ragged shorts was nothing like her father. He leaned back in his seat, smiling contentedly.

"Glad you're here, Chloe."

"Me, too," she answered.

❧

After her conversation with Uncle Howard in the pilothouse, Chloe made her way along the starboard side of the boat to the aft deck. Jennifer was still sitting at the table with a book open before her. She was alone, and Chloe wondered where the other student went. She approached Jennifer, hoping to learn a little more of what to expect from this excursion.

Jennifer closed her book as Chloe sat across from her. "Did you finish unpacking?" she asked.

Chloe shrugged. "Not really. But I'm sure there will be more time later." She noticed Jennifer's arms were already turning a light shade of pink.

Jennifer's gaze followed Chloe's. "Don't worry about me. I have plenty of sunscreen on. I always get a little burned every time I get on a boat."

"How many of these expeditions have you gone on?" Chloe asked.

"This will be my second—first time at sea with Professor Gary. I've never tracked a turtle before or been on a boat this nice. The last expedition hung around in Texas waters as we studied the feeding habits of the turtles."

"Have you worked with Gary on any other projects?"

"Yes, a year ago. I was on the rescue team for injured turtles, and Gary headed up the team. Working with him is a unique experience. He's like a mama grizzly bear. Very proud and protective of what's important to him. Growls a lot. Temperamental. Perfectionist. He's also very knowledge-able and gets excited over his work. Everybody has a different opinion of him. I think he's okay. He has a soft side to him."

"Who's the other student on this trip?" Chloe asked, eager to change the subject. She didn't want to appear too inter-ested in Gary.

"That's Brent Parker. He's worked on several projects with Professor Gary—even traveled with him in his studies. I'm surprised you haven't met Brent yet. He's probably up on the flybridge working on his tan. He loves this boat."

Something in the way Jennifer said Brent's name told Chloe he was special to her. "He's your boyfriend?"

"No!" Color fused Jennifer's pale cheeks. "He's just a really good-looking and funny guy. He doesn't even know I exist."

"I find that hard to believe since you're on the same boat together."

"Yeah, well, he'd never show interest in a girl like me. Last semester he was dating one of the cheerleaders. I couldn't fit one leg in those tiny skirts. You could wear one, though. I think I weigh twice as much as you do."

Chloe shrugged, feeling like the conversation had taken an odd turn. "I wouldn't care to fit into one of those skirts. Besides, who cares how much you weigh? The world may compare people to anorexic models, but the right guy won't judge you by the number on the scale. He'll see the real treasure in you."

Jennifer stared at Chloe as she considered her words. "I'd really like to think you're right," she finally said. There was an unmistakable wistfulness in her voice.

"Me, too," Chloe added to herself.

Gary peeked his head out through the sliding door. "There you are!" He gave her and Jennifer an engaging smile. "Will you come in so we can have our first meeting? We need to go over shipboard rules." He spoke as though there was never a dispute between himself and Chloe.

Chloe rose from her seat. If he could pretend like nothing was wrong then so could she. God would want her to forgive him, and she would. But trusting him was a different story.

Inside, Jennifer and Chloe settled on the leather sofa with Gary seated in a recliner across from them. A tall, gangly young man crossed the salon and sat in the recliner adjacent to Gary. With a confident grin at Gary he popped open his can of soda and took a long drink.

"Let's get started," Gary said, clapping his hands together. Suddenly he was all business, going over the details of the trip and what he expected from each of them. "We're going to be working closely together the next few weeks so first I want you to meet Chloe."

"I know Chloe from taking her literature class last year," Jennifer chimed in.

Brent stood and crossed over to Chloe. He gave her a firm handshake, holding her hand longer than necessary. "It's good to meet you, Chloe. I'm Brent Parker."

"Hello, Brent," Chloe answered while subtly trying to extract her hand from his grasp.

"If you'll take a seat, Brent, we'll continue," Gary interrupted. He appeared less than amused by Brent's chivalry.

Brent took his seat, but his gaze remained on Chloe. At first Chloe thought she was imagining his admiration, but his gaze didn't waver. Chloe glanced at Jennifer to see if she noticed Brent's behavior. Jennifer was staring at Gary with rapt attention. And Gary was focused on his discussion about sea turtle tracking.

"Brent and Jennifer, we'll each take turns tracking Daisy. The information we receive from the tracking system will need to be given to Howard. But for the most part he'll follow a set course to Rancho Nuevo, the turtle nesting beach."

Chloe glanced at Brent to find him looking at her again. When he caught her glancing at him, he gave her a flirty wink. Chloe quickly turned away, an uncomfortable blush rising to her cheeks. Silence filled the room. Chloe looked up to find Gary scowling at Brent.

"As long as everyone is paying attention, let's continue this meeting. We'll each take a turn in the kitchen. Who wants to go fir—"

Before Gary could finish both Jennifer and Brent called out, "Not me!" All gazes turned to Chloe who sat in bewilderment.

"I think what these two kids are trying to say is that they don't want us to suffer from their lack of cooking ability.

Would you care to take lunch today, Chloe? It would save us from Brent's peanut butter and jelly sandwiches."

Put like that, how could she refuse? "Okay. I'll do my best to avoid making PB and Js," Chloe offered uncertainly. "But I don't plan to take all the meals," she added. She didn't want any of them to think that she was the ship's cook. She signed on as chaperone—then added secretary to the list of responsibilities. She wasn't about to become the cook on top of everything else!

Gary gave her an appreciative smile that Chloe couldn't possibly consider insincere. When he looked at her in such a way, she could almost think he liked her. It was as though he had never been frustrated with her or said insulting things. If only they had just met. They never would have dated or broken up. This trip could be a starting point for them without memories. She might have let herself explore a relationship with him. But there was no relationship here, she reminded herself. He was Gary Erickson, the man who'd crushed her dreams. And she was a chaperone and secretary for the trip. Nothing more. Even if he was attractive and a Christian, there were no relationship possibilities. Period. Keep your thoughts on track, Chloe!

"And last I want to talk to you about computer privileges," Gary continued. "Since we'll be on board for several weeks, we'll primarily use the laptop via satellite to stay connected with the rest of the world. We use technology similar to what's used on cruise ships. This is expensive, so no boredom surfing on the Web, please. And no phone calls from the boat unless we're docked and have a landline. I'll set up E-mail accounts for each of you, and you can contact your friends and family through E-mail. I also have a Web site where we'll keep track of our findings. I plan to upload pictures and record data on this site. University students will be able to track us through the site as well as contact us with any questions they might have.

"Chloe will be using the laptop to record data, so don't let any online socializing interfere with her work. Also, keep in mind that this is a privately owned yacht. Howard Statton has cut the university quite a deal in taking us to Mexico. Treat this boat better than your own homes."

He paused, making sure Jennifer and Brent understood what he was saying. "First stop will be South Padre Island before we head south to Mexico. Chloe, if you wouldn't mind putting something together for lunch now, I know we'd all appreciate it."

Brent jumped to his feet. "I'd be happy to help Chloe with lunch," he offered with a wink in Chloe's direction.

Gary gave him a playful yet firm push toward the doors that led to the aft deck. "You can have cooking lessons another time, Brent. Right now I need you to check the diving equipment."

Gary, Jennifer, and Brent scooted out of the salon, leaving Chloe on her own in the galley. She watched their retreat with dismay. How did she get cornered into being the first cook? It was because she wanted to be nice and please them. Well, she agreed to do it so there was no sense complaining about it. But she would be sure somebody else took the dinner shift.

She peered in several of the cabinets, taking stock of her supplies. She expected to find the basics like peanut butter and jelly, but there was so much more. In one cabinet she found caviar. The freezer held T-bone steaks, frozen vegetables, and even two boxed pizzas. There were ripe fruits, different types of cheese, and a variety of other fresh items. There were more supplies than Chloe anticipated finding on a boat. Gary didn't have to worry about peanut butter and jelly. Chloe whipped together fresh fruit smoothies, thick tuna sandwiches with tomato and lettuce, and big, juicy pickles on the side.

Once she was finished preparing the food, Chloe wondered if everyone expected to be served or called. After a moment of indecision Chloe grabbed a plate to take to Uncle Howard in the pilothouse. When she came back to the galley she found Brent's and Jennifer's plates missing. Gary was eating while he stared at a map of the Gulf of Mexico. His fruit drink was gone, and the sandwich was quickly following suit. He didn't even step aside or look up when she reached past him to clean up the kitchen mess.

"We'll dock later at South Padre Island. They had a pretty good nesting record of green sea turtles this year. We'll do some diving near the island before leaving to go farther south."

"Diving? As in scuba?" she asked, her voice betraying her excitement.

Gary nodded. "I don't remember you being interested in diving. Are you certified?"

"Yes. Since last summer. I've always wanted to dive for sunken ships." Chloe would have continued, but Gary didn't seem to be listening.

"Is it getting warm in here?" he asked suddenly.

Chloe looked at him closely. A crimson flush was rising up his neck and tiny red spots broke out on his face. "Are you okay?"

"I don't feel like myself." He closed his eyes as he reached for the nearest chair. "It just came on me suddenly." He opened his eyes and focused on Chloe's face.

"Could it be the stress? You've been working hard to get everything ready," Chloe suggested. Their earlier argument was forgotten as she stared at him in concern.

Gary's gaze rested on the glass of fruit smoothie that Chloe held. "What did you put in that?"

Chloe shrugged. "Several things—strawberries, kiwi, bananas, and lemonade. I was surprised at how much we have stocked. We won't be stuck with peanut butter and jelly sandwiches for every meal."

"Did you say bananas?" Gary said hoarsely.

Chloe nodded. "Bananas, strawberries, kiwi—"

"I'm allergic to bananas!" Gary fiercely scratched at his arms. "Look at me!"

His arms and legs were breaking out in hundreds of minuscule red bumps. "I'm getting hot. It must have been loaded with bananas for me to react this bad. I'm turning into one big hive!" He started rummaging through several of the crates stacked under the table. "Where's the calamine lotion? Augh!"

"Are you breathing okay?" Chloe asked as she helped him search through the boxes. Allergies could easily affect breathing, and she definitely didn't want to deal with a respiratory emergency out in the middle of the ocean!

"Yes, I'm breathing fine!" Gary growled. "Just let me know if you find the lotion. I'm going outside."

Chloe wanted to warn him that the sun might aggravate his condition. Yet with his current state of mind she didn't dare say anything. Instead she continued to look for the calamine lotion, determined to set things right.

Ten minutes later Chloe found the first aid box in the pilothouse. Jennifer told her that Gary had gone down to his cabin because the sun was bothering him. Chloe refrained from having any "I told you so" thoughts as she went to find him.

She knocked on his stateroom door and stepped into the cabin when he bid her to enter. The room was different than hers. It was smaller, with wide bunk beds built into the wall. Gary was stretched out on the bottom bed with his eyes closed. His hands were behind his head, and he looked comfortable except for the angry rash covering every visible spot of his skin.

"I found the lotion," Chloe said softly. Her voice trembled on the words.

Gary opened his eyes and gazed at her.

"I'm sorry about the bananas. I didn't know. If I had known, I wouldn't have. . ." Chloe cut herself off, spreading her hands helplessly.

"You didn't know. Chloe, I'm sorry for sounding like such an idiot. I didn't mean to yell at you."

Chloe handed him the lotion then turned to leave. She paused in the doorway. "Would you like me to pray with you?"

Silence stretched, and Chloe wasn't sure Gary was going to respond.

"You would do that for me? Even after the way I growled at you? Even after—well, everything?"

"Of course."

A slow, uncharacteristic smile spread over his face. "Thanks, Chloe. You don't have to, but I appreciate the thought. I think I'll be just fine."

As Chloe went back up to the galley she whispered a prayer on Gary's behalf anyway. Feeling confident that God would take care of him, Chloe settled herself in front of the computer. When it came to dealing with people or computers, she preferred computers. She didn't have to worry about saying or doing the right thing. If things went wrong, all she had to do was reboot. Dealing with Gary wasn't as easy as rebooting a computer, by any means. He was a complicated person. He was attractive—just the sight of him made her pulse skip. But then he opened his mouth and spoiled everything. Or she did something wrong, and the tension grew between them.

Her thoughts were focused on Gary as she stared at the

blank computer screen. She barely noticed the sliding door open.

"Say cheese!" Brent popped in, flashing the digital camera in Chloe's face.

"Why did you do that?" Chloe demanded crossly.

"Sorry, Chloe. I didn't mean to upset you." He shifted his weight from one foot to the other, his expression puzzled. He didn't look like the cocky college boy any longer. Chloe felt like she had wounded him with her harsh reaction.

She consciously softened her tone. "Why are you taking pictures of me? I'm sure you can find a better subject worthy of the film."

Brent graced her with an award-winning smile. "I can't find anyone that I'd rather take pictures of. Ever think of doing a little modeling? I'm thinking about going into photography, and you'll be the model to send my career through the roof."

Chloe groaned. "You've got to be kidding. Brent, go tease someone else." She really wasn't in the mood for any childish antics.

Brent looked offended. "I wasn't teasing! You're beautiful!" He moved close enough to tug on her ponytail. "You just need the right guy telling you how wonderful you are."

Chloe leaned away from him. "I must not have met the right guy yet. The men I know tell me how wonderful they are." She paused as Brent perched himself on the arm of her chair. She tried to pretend his closeness didn't bother her. "So tell me the real reason you're taking pictures."

"For the Web site. It's all finished except for pictures of the crew. As we journey forward, I'll add different pictures every day or so. I'll make you a star!" He leaned nearer until Chloe got a strong whiff of his cologne. She could easily count the freckles across his nose and see the brown flecks in his hazel eyes. "What are you doing on the computer?" he asked.

Chloe snatched at the neutral topic as though it were a lifeline. "Nothing yet, but I need to get to work. I have to figure out these computer programs before Professor Gary gives me his notes. It's amazing how this entire trip is focused around the assumed destination of one turtle. And from the data collected so far, it looks like their estimations are correct. I'm trying to learn everything I can about this sea turtle program so I'll be up to speed."

Brent shrugged with disinterest. "Yeah, well, I really don't get into the technical stuff. It's an easy credit for me, and I get to spend a few weeks on a boat. Want to go out on deck so I can take more pictures of you?"

His nonchalance surprised Chloe. She expected everyone on this expedition to be as enthusiastic as Gary. Brent's lack of exuberance was disappointing. Or maybe he was trying to appear casual just to impress her. Surely Gary wouldn't select a student who didn't really care about the project. "I don't think so, Brent. I want to go over some more of Professor Gary's notes from his last project." She was relieved when he finally rose from the arm of her chair.

"We'll be stopping at South Padre Island soon. They have a neat little turtle rescue place there. But the beach is even better. Maybe you and I could play in the waves."

Chloe didn't bother answering. Brent was a flirt, and she was sure he didn't intend a word of it. "See you later, Brent," she called absently.

three

We're ready to go down. Everyone, get suited up!" Gary bellowed.

Chloe heard Gary's shout but didn't respond. Instead, she sipped her hot tea as she sat on the sofa next to her uncle.

She had expected they would dock at the marina of South Padre Island and have time to tour the town. Instead, the boat was anchored about a mile south of the island. She had heard so many things about South Padre—mostly that it was the spring break party capital. The beaches were supposed to be beautiful. There were dozens of gift shops and restaurants—even a water park. And she wasn't going to see any of it because Gary had no intention of stopping at the island. He only wanted to take a short dive to make sure all their gear was in optimal working condition before they left the States and headed into Mexican waters.

"Have you spent much time at South Padre Island?" Chloe asked Uncle Howard.

He popped open a can of soda. "Some. It's a nice place. Busy during the summer months. There are some incredible vacation homes right off the beach."

"Chloe!" Gary bellowed from outside.

Chloe gave her uncle an apologetic smile. "Duty calls."

When Gary barked her name again, Chloe hurried to the aft deck, wondering what she had done this time. By the tone of Gary's voice, she was once again in the wrong place at the wrong time. What was it with men? She couldn't please them, and she definitely couldn't understand them. Lord, help me understand this man. I can't work with someone who yells and gets mad all the time. Chloe stiffened her shoulders and stepped outside.

"You called?" she asked, mustering all the patience she could.

"Hollered is more like it," Brent quipped.

Gary didn't respond. Instead, he hefted two air tanks to the diving platform. Both he and Brent were preparing for their dive. Once he set the tanks down he turned to Chloe. "Brent's right. I'm sorry about yelling."

Chloe nodded, surprised by the sudden apology.

"Why aren't you suited up? Don't you want to go down?" He studied her shorts and T-shirt with a frown.

"I didn't know you wanted me to. I'm sorry. I'll change right away," she stammered under Gary's steady gaze.

Down in her quarters, Chloe changed into her simple blue bathing suit. It took longer than it should have because she was nervous and her fumbling fingers wouldn't cooperate. Gary was waiting, and she was sure the longer he waited, the less congenial he would be. The turtles wouldn't wait forever and neither would Professor Erickson!

Back up on deck Chloe found Gary and Brent already suited up, each with an air tank strapped to his back and mask over his face. Jennifer lugged another air tank to the edge of the boat. "Here, Chloe; let me help you with this." She handed Chloe fins and a mask. With one last check of the gauge on the air tank, Jennifer turned to Chloe and helped her lift it to her back.

"You're not going?" Chloe asked as she adjusted the mask.

"No. I'm not certified yet. But I'll be down there one of these days. Keep an eye out for turtles. It's really grassy in this spot, and the green sea turtles love that for feeding. Unfortunately, in busy areas they get hit by boats or tangled in fishing line."

"Let's go, Chloe! We're growing old here!" Brent complained.

Chloe's sigh of exasperation didn't go unnoticed by Jennifer. "He's excited. Don't mind him."

"I know. I'm trying to be patient with these men, but it isn't easy."

Chloe joined Gary and Brent at the dive platform. The waves seemed big to Chloe. She had to concentrate on keeping her footing on the platform as the swells gently rocked the boat. Together they fell backward into the water and were instantly submerged in another world. The current gently pushed at Chloe. It took her a moment to adjust to her new surroundings. Once the bubbles cleared enough for her to see, she was able to spot Brent and Gary. They were already diving deeper, swimming toward the long sea grass at the bottom.

As Chloe swam closer, she caught sight of a small green sea turtle. Its shell was about eighteen inches in diameter. It ripped into the grass, stirring up the small fish that were hiding. Chloe continued to watch as different fish darted past, some silver, others a dull gray with darker stripes. Slowly she caught up to the men who were pointing to an odd formation of wood and sand several yards away. Chloe caught her breath. It was her first shipwreck!

Ignoring the men, she swam straight for the sunken boat. It wasn't anything much—a small yacht. It was partially buried in the sand and lying on its side. Fish swam in and out through the broken windows. The boat wasn't as old as Chloe first imagined, and she wondered what caused it to be a sunken wreck. It was murky inside the boat, but she could make out some items in the mess. A chair, broken dishes. . .a large beer keg was wedged under the anchored table. Something unusual caught Chloe's attention, and she went in for a closer look.

There's a turtle in that wreck. Why would a turtle be in there? Chloe dove deeper until she could peer inside the cabin from a different angle. She spied piles of fishing nets. And trapped in one of the nets was a large turtle.

I'm going in. If it stays in there too long, it'll die. Then a thought struck her. Perhaps the turtle was already dead. She watched it for a few seconds, willing it to move. As she waited, the poor turtle kicked its front flippers, wrestling to be free. The efforts weren't much. It must have been trapped for some time.

Chloe decided the best way to get into the wrecked yacht was through one of the broken windows. It was probably the same way the turtle got in. Just as she grasped the window frame someone grabbed her arm. Chloe let out a shriek and dozens of bubbles flooded her vision. Gary stared at her through his mask. He vigorously shook his head.

Chloe pointed at the trapped turtle. Gary peered inside the yacht then nodded excitedly when he spotted the turtle. He reached for the window frame and carefully pushed himself through the opening. With gentle strokes he paddled toward the entangled turtle. Chloe watched from her vantage point at the window, willing Gary to hurry. He pulled out the knife that was strapped to his belt then quickly cut the turtle loose. Chloe expected the turtle to dart away once it was free, but it remained motionless. Gary had to move it. He pushed the exhausted turtle through the window and into Chloe's hands. The turtle was bigger than she first thought. Its shell was brownish with jagged edges. She guessed it to be two feet from head to tail.

Gary pulled himself back through the window and gently took the turtle out of Chloe's hands. Chloe pointed toward the surface—Gary nodded in agreement. He took off at a quick pace with tight, strong kicks. Chloe looked to see where Brent was. He, too, was heading to the surface.

By the time Chloe caught up with the men, Brent was

already out of the water, and Gary was handing the injured turtle to him. Together Brent and Jennifer managed to get the turtle onto the dive platform.

Gary climbed out of the water and held out his hand to help Chloe.

"Is it going to be okay?" Chloe asked as Gary pulled her onto the boat.

"It's difficult to say. But thanks to you, he has a better chance now than he did trapped in that net."

"Why do you think he went into that wreck?"

"Who knows? Maybe he saw something shiny or mistook the nets for a food source. Or perhaps he swam in there to escape a predator."

Uncle Howard came out back to share in the discovery. "Nice-sized turtle. I haven't seen one of those type of turtles in a long time." He pointed at the rough brown edges of the turtle's shell.

Chloe unloaded her scuba gear onto the rack and reached for a towel. Brent and Gary also shed their gear and were squatting over the turtle. The turtle didn't move.

"Is he going to be all right?" she asked Brent.

"He's fine," Gary answered before Brent could comment. "His breathing is steady. He just seems to be tired." Gary checked the turtle for other injuries. Slowly the turtle flapped its front flippers. "Jennifer, help me tag him, then we'll release him."

As Jennifer scooted away to do Gary's bidding, Gary peered at Chloe. "Good job spotting him. Our first rescue this trip, and he wasn't even stranded on a beach. You get the privilege, Chloe, of naming him." He rewarded her with one of his rare full smiles.

"Name him? What do you name turtles?" she paused, feeling self-conscious yet extremely pleased with Gary's praise. "I guess I could name him Champ." She shrugged uncertainly.

Brent put his arm around Chloe's shoulders and gave her a fun-loving squeeze. "I think Champ is a great name. He's a fighter, and he's going to overcome! Good choice, Chloe." He pulled Chloe closer until she was tucked neatly against his side. He then planted a friendly kiss on top of her head. Jennifer returned with the tagging supplies in time to witness Brent's flirting. She looked like she was about to cry. Gary seemed furious. And her uncle was turning red with suppressed laughter.

Chloe nudged herself away from Brent, uncomfortable with the stares she received from the others. "I think I'll go change. Be right back," she mumbled. She scooted away from Brent and hurried into the cabin.

Gary was quick on her heels and cornered her in the small hallway between the staterooms. "Is there something between you and Brent that I should be aware of?" He glared at Chloe, waiting for her to answer.

"Brent and me? You've got to be joking!" His accusation was laughable, but Gary wasn't smiling. "I can't believe you would suggest such a thing."

"I'm not providing a floating dating service. I expect you to maintain your professionalism on board as you would in the classroom. If you're interested in Brent, save it for next term. Don't do it on my time."

Angry tears filled Chloe's eyes. Why was it her fault? She hadn't done anything to encourage Brent. In fact, she'd gone out of her way to avoid his flirtations. Had Gary talked to Brent about his behavior, or was he blaming it all on Chloe?

"If you still knew me, you would realize how wrong you are," Chloe whispered. "Now please let me change in my room, Professor Erickson. We're making a watery mess of this hallway."

As Gary looked down to survey the mess they were making, Chloe slipped into her room and shut the door with a firm snap.

If Chloe hadn't been soaking wet she would have thrown herself on the bed for a good cry. Instead she sagged to the floor, allowing her tears to mingle with the water dripping from her hair.

The excitement over finding and rescuing the tangled turtle was now gone. It amazed Chloe that Gary blamed her for Brent's flirtations. Brent was harmless—annoying, but not threatening. And she chose to ignore him. His obvious interest was irritating, and she didn't welcome it. Couldn't Gary see she didn't have feelings for Brent? And now, how could she face any of them? If Gary thought she was a shameless flirt, then what did Jennifer think? Surely the girl would see the truth that Gary had missed. Chloe would never deliberately hurt Jennifer.

"Lord, please show me how to fix this," she whispered. Just talking to the Lord and knowing He didn't find fault with her was comforting. "I knew that Gary would be difficult to work with, but I had no idea this situation would come up. I feel so angry with him that if I weren't stuck on this boat right now I would quit this job. I know I need to forgive him. I don't even think I like him. Help me, Lord, to work this out."

Chloe felt better after she prayed and more in control of her emotions. She knew the first thing she needed to do was to find Jennifer and make sure there weren't any misunderstandings. As for Gary, she would leave him to God's dealings. When it came to Gary Erickson, she couldn't do anything right. It was best for her to steer clear of him.

Chloe found Jennifer sitting at the table on the aft deck. Gary and Brent were nowhere in sight. Chloe breathed a sigh a relief. At least she could talk to Jennifer without anyone else around. "Jennifer, can I talk to you for a minute?"

Jennifer visibly stiffened. "Professor Gary released Champ. The turtle disappeared as soon as he was dropped into the water. I think he'll do just fine."

Chloe sat at the table across from Jennifer. "He looked different than the other turtles I've seen. His shell seemed rougher than the green sea turtles, and he was a different color than the Kemp's ridley. Is he a different kind?" It was difficult to talk about the turtle when all she wanted to do was clear up the mess between them, but Jennifer seemed determined to keep it professional. Somehow, though, Chloe resolved to clear the air between them.

"Hawksbill. They're hunted for their shells, and that's why this species is so rare." Silence fell between Chloe and Jennifer.

"I'm not after Brent," Chloe said, changing the subject to the problem at hand. Chloe knew Jennifer was upset even though she feigned otherwise.

Jennifer shrugged. "It's okay if you want to go out with him. I don't have a claim on him," she said casually.

Chloe knew Jennifer wasn't as disinterested as she pretended to be. "I haven't encouraged him. Please believe me. He's a student at the university where I teach. Nothing more. Besides, my life is much less complicated without men. I'd just as soon live without them."

"Why don't you like men? I've noticed you try to stay away from both Gary and Brent, but your uncle doesn't bother you—because he's family, I'm sure."

It was Chloe's turn to be evasive. She toyed with her ponytail, wishing she could change the subject again. She didn't want to tell anyone about her prior involvement with Gary. If that bit of news got around campus it would be embarrassing. Besides, it was a part of her life she'd like to forget. "It's a long, boring story. I've just learned through hard lessons that

I can't find the right man who values what's important. So it's best to avoid them all. And Uncle Howard understands me. That's why we don't have a problem."

Jennifer nodded as though she understood exactly what Chloe had said. "Thanks for telling me, Chloe. I know I shouldn't have been jealous of you. It's just hard to see Brent interested in other women when I want to be the one he cares for. I'm not surprised he turned to you, though. You're cute and little. Just the type he's always drawn to."

"He's about twenty, isn't he?" she asked, and Jennifer nodded. "Trust me, Jennifer. Brent will get the idea. He thinks he can flash that smile and every girl will melt. I'm too old for that. And I'm tired of women being manipulated by self-centered men," she added, hoping her last comment sounded less personal than it was.

Jennifer gave her a sympathetic look. "And you need the one man that recognizes the treasure within you."

Gary's image came to Chloe's mind, but she quickly pressed it away. She was glad Jennifer remembered her encouraging words. But she didn't want to think about men anymore. Her record with men was a disaster, and her troubles with Gary proved she couldn't get it right. He was angry with her again. What she had was a boss who was waiting in the wings for her to make a mistake so he could pounce. And if she didn't make a mistake, he concocted one on her behalf. If only all men had the likeness of her Heavenly Father. All men were created in His image, but they sure didn't act like Him.

"If you don't need me to do anything, I'm going to send an E-mail off to my mom. I know she's curious about what I've been doing."

Jennifer nodded. "Go right ahead. I'm going to log on later tonight. I'm so glad we can keep in contact with family through E-mail."

Chloe went into the empty salon and settled in front of the laptop computer. There was a list of assigned E-mail addresses next to the computer. She quickly logged into her personal E-mail account. There was already an E-mail from Professor Erickson. Chloe quickly skimmed the note. It was a brief reminder to all of them of computer time limits and acceptable Internet usage.

"As usual, he's all business," Chloe muttered. After deleting the message Chloe began a quick note to her mom. She told her about finding Champ in the shipwreck, her tiny cabin, and working with Jennifer. She suddenly felt an intense longing to see her mom and talk to her. She wanted to tell her about how Gary accused her and grumbled at her. It was more than she could explain through an electronic note.

Just as she was about to log off she noticed another E-mail. The sender's address was unfamiliar. Then she remembered that Gary put their E-mail addresses on the Web site so students at the university could track their voyage and contact them.

Dear Chloe,

I just wanted to tell you I'm sorry. I've never been good at communicating my true feelings and often I say the opposite of what I mean. So, needless to say, I find this form of communication much easier than speaking. I just wanted to tell you that I'm not the terrible person you think I am, even though I haven't given you reason to believe otherwise. Having you here has turned me inside out. I can't think straight, and I guess I react harshly to you because I don't know how to talk to you anymore. You're beautiful and kind, and Brent has every reason to be attracted to you. Please forgive me for being so tough on you. There are so many more things to say, but now is not the time to get into them. Suffice it to say I'm a work in progress, and God has a long way to go on me.

Yours truly,
Gary

Chloe read the E-mail three times. Gary's honesty surprised her. It wasn't typical for the man to apologize, yet here was another apology from Gary. It was impossible to stay mad after such a heartfelt plea. Of course she would forgive him. Actually, she already had forgiven him. It was so much easier to let it go quickly than to allow the offense to grow. She wondered how she should respond to his note. She could go find him and tell him that she forgave him, yet that might be awkward for both of them. A quick message sent back through E-mail was probably the best answer. Taking a deep breath, Chloe began her response. She needed to keep it light and impersonal. Professional. That would be the best.

Dear Gary,
  Thank you for writing to me. I accept your apology, though I don't agree that Brent has reason to be attracted me. The last thing I ever wanted was his attention. I hope, despite all the misunderstandings, we'll have a good working relationship from this point on.

Sincerely,
Chloe

Chloe reread her response several times before getting up the courage to send it. It sounded sincere yet professional, and she hoped Gary would get the underlying message in her brief statements. She wasn't interested in Brent. Period. She didn't want to find herself in any more difficult situations.

"Chloe."

She jumped at the sound of her name and flushed when she

realized it was Gary who had called her.

"I need you to transcribe this dictation." He handed her a small cassette recorder and a floppy disk. "You can use the laptop while I'm working on the other PC. Save it on this disk."

His tone was friendly yet impersonal, and Chloe wondered what he was thinking. He didn't know she'd already read his message. Perhaps he thought she was still angry with him. She opened her mouth to say she forgave him—it was no big deal—but the words wouldn't come. Instead, she wordlessly took the recorder and turned back to the computer. He would have to read the message she sent. Then he would understand. Gary didn't move away as Chloe began transcribing his notes. His presence made her jumpy, and she kept hitting the wrong keys. Ignore him and get down to business! Chloe chastised herself.

Soon she was lost in her work, listening to the amazing information Gary had formulated thus far on their journey. He included information about Champ that she never would have noticed. He knew Champ was a male by the length of his tale. He identified several scars on the shell and flippers, possibly caused by predators. All Chloe had seen in her brief moments with the turtle were that he was big and different from the other sea turtles she'd seen. The observations were fascinating and Chloe absorbed everything as she typed. She didn't even remember that Gary was reading over her shoulder.

"You do a remarkable job. Mrs. Phipps never underlined or put key info into boxes. That looks really nice."

Chloe flushed at his praise and was glad he couldn't see her face. "Thank you, Gary." She kept her voice purposely unaffected and professional.

"I talked with Brent. I hope we'll have smooth sailing from here on out."

Chloe straightened at Gary's inference of the so-called romance between herself and Brent. "You never had anything to worry about in the first place," she murmured. She turned to look up at Gary. He was much closer to her than she expected. She scooted her chair forward, enlarging the distance between them.

"I'm not so sure. Brent and Jennifer have worked with me together before, and I've never had a problem. I've certainly never had any troubles with Mrs. Phipps except that she grumbled at me every chance she got. Then you come along, and I have new dynamics to deal with."

Chloe wanted to retort that if Brent were not so consumed with physical appearances, Gary would have friendly issues to deal with between Jennifer and Brent. How could Gary not see that Jennifer pined for Brent? She watched his every move, laughed too loudly at his stupid jokes, and hung on his every word.

Chloe, however, would like to put Brent in the dinghy and pull him behind the boat. Then she wouldn't have to deal with his flirting.

"Are you saying I'm the problem?" Chloe asked softly. Was he accusing her again? He must not have meant a word of his written apology if he was already blaming her for Brent's behavior again. This was worse than she could have imagined. He made her suffer six years without him. Then he accused her and harassed her every chance he got. She never should have come on this excursion. Trevor had been right, though he knew nothing about Gary Erickson.

"I'm just saying I never expected to need a chaperone for my chaperone." His words were lightly spoken, but they stung just the same.

Chloe willed her voice to stay strong as she answered him. "If I'm such a problem for you, let me go. I'll get off the boat in Brownsville, rent a car, and be home late tonight. You won't have any more dynamics to deal with."

Gary shook his head. "It isn't that easy. I need you to chaperone. You can't bail out at the first sign of trouble. You have to see this through—we both do."

"You're a fine one to accuse me of running! You ditched me, remember? I'm just giving you the option that if you don't like me, I'll leave!"

"It's obviously not a matter of what I like or dislike. It's a matter of keeping you and Brent away from each other so we can keep the peace."

Chloe couldn't believe the nerve of this man! Why couldn't he just drop the matter? Instead he had to run it into the ground that he didn't want her with Brent. Well, fine! As far as I'm concerned, there aren't any men on this boat except my uncle! Professor Gary Erickson has no idea how professional I can be!

"Is that all, Professor Erickson? You've made your point abundantly clear. I will no longer throw myself at Brent or you or any other male that crosses my path during this trip. I'll do my best to contain my hopelessly feminine flirtations. You won't have another problem with me, Professor!" She scooted her chair back in front of the laptop and started tapping furiously at the keys. Her vision blurred with tears, and she wasn't even sure what she was typing.

Gary's groan was one of frustration. "That's not what I meant—Chloe, please. It's just that. . ."

Chloe's fingers paused on the keyboard, but she didn't turn around. She waited for him to continue. He owed her a huge apology, and hopefully he realized that fact. Silence stretched.

"Forget it," he finally said. "I'll let you get back to work."

Chloe's shoulders sagged in disappointment. What did it matter? Gary was abrasive and judgmental. His apology was worthless. He only saw what he wanted, not the truth. Whenever he spoke to her, she was left feeling bruised. If she could swim better, she would jump ship and head to shore. She'd do anything to get away from this terrible situation.

Why hadn't God warned her before she agreed to chaperone? By the end of the excursion Gary would probably have trampled every tender emotion she possessed.

four

Bright light blinded Chloe as she came out on deck the next morning. She had spent a terrible night tossing in her bed. She was glad she and Jennifer had their own rooms. Otherwise, Jennifer wouldn't have slept a wink. All night Chloe worried about her working relationship with Gary. She didn't know how she could please him. Then she thought about her failure to please him six years ago. If she couldn't make him happy then, how did she think it possible to do so now? Those thoughts led her to think about Trevor. She knew Trevor was at home waiting for her to come crawling back in failure. She felt like a failure. More than once she wanted to quit and find a way home, but she couldn't do that. Somehow, she had to draw on the strength God had placed in her. She had to overcome the difficulties. She couldn't return home a quitter. Trevor would gloat, her father would grumble at her for wasting time, and she would feel terrible. No, she wouldn't quit no matter how much she displeased Gary. The joy of the Lord was her strength!

"Morning," Brent greeted as she approached the group sitting around the table on the aft deck. Chloe gave him a wan smile and slipped her sunglasses onto her nose. She forced a smile in Gary's direction as well. He nodded in response but didn't say anything.

It's just as well he doesn't say anything to me. He's said more than enough, and the trip has barely begun. He probably regrets asking me to come as much as I regret it accepting the job.

"We're discussing Daisy's approximate destination," Jennifer explained. "She's suddenly taken a turn away from the path we'd predicted she would take to the nesting beach. She seems to be heading back north rather than south to nest as we expected."

Chloe peered at the chart spread out on the table. The last two recordings of her location showed Daisy retracing her path.

"What if she doesn't turn south again? What does it mean for this trip?" Chloe asked. Perhaps her sleepless night was for nothing. If the turtle didn't nest, then the trip would be canceled. She could go home, forgetting this grand adventure.

"We continue to Rancho Nuevo," Gary answered stiffly. "Regardless of what Daisy does, we will study the nesting of the Kemp's ridleys at the beach. I've got permission to bring eggs back with us for transplanting on a beach in Texas. Whether Daisy arrives at the beach or not won't alter our research expedition." He pressed his lips into a grim line, and his gaze locked with Chloe's. She knew he thought she was trying to quit again. Well, he was right! She was disappointed she had to continue with this excursion. Chloe met Gary's gaze evenly, challenging him to say more disparaging remarks. Several emotions flitted through his light eyes, and she was surprised to see regret settle into his gaze. She steeled herself against any reaction. She wouldn't care this time! He was just like Trevor and her father. He didn't really care about her feelings.

❧

The Texas shoreline quickly blended into Mexico as they traveled along the coast. The farther south they went, the higher the temperature climbed. Fortunately the breeze was cool, keeping the weather comfortable. Everyone went to different parts of the boat once the meeting was over. Jennifer claimed to have too much sun exposure already and opted to stay inside. Brent wanted to watch a movie in the salon, and Gary grumbled something about more work to tend to. Chloe climbed the stairs to the empty flybridge, the top deck above the salon. The view of sparkling waves was wonderful, and she sat on one of the starboard benches to enjoy the view. The gentle rocking of the boat was soothing. She felt peaceful, and the sun warmed her face. Chloe could understand why Uncle Howard enjoyed owning The Bounty and going to all the tropical ports. It was a unique world of its own.

Chloe's reverie was broken when Gary appeared on the deck. She pretended not to notice him as he moved to the rail. She observed him from behind her dark glasses as he stood staring out over the water. She was struck again by what a handsome man he was. His sun-bleached hair waved in the breeze. She noticed he needed a shave. He seemed perfectly at home in shorts and a T-shirt, with white sunscreen smattered across his nose. Somehow, she couldn't recall the image of him she had carried with her for the past six years. Though he hadn't changed greatly, the changes were there nevertheless. And she much preferred the man he had become.

Chloe thought about all their misunderstandings, starting with the breakup. Gary had delivered some pretty harsh comments to Chloe that still stung when she thought about them. The recent accusations over Brent were the most offensive. Did he think she was a flirt as he insinuated? The comments rang as ridiculous and unfounded. Imagine me being accused of flirting! She wouldn't know the first thing about trying to gain a man's attention. She didn't know how to flirt, and she didn't want to know! Her lack of boyfriends wasn't due to her appearance, though she'd never win any beauty contests. She felt her thick, dark hair was pleasant. It softened her appearance because it was a warm and rich brown that flowed gently to her shoulders. And her eyes—the color of cocoa—were her best feature. But did she think she was a boy magnet, screaming for attention? That was laughable.

When Gary stopped beside her and sat down, she realized she'd been so lost in thought she hadn't seen him leave the railing.

"Are you enjoying the trip so far?" he asked. His words came out stiff.

Chloe guessed he was making an effort at being pleasant. She didn't feel so generous. "You mean when I'm not on my manhunt?" she asked. Immediately she wished she could snatch back the petty words.

Gary stiffened. "Listen, you don't have to be that way. I'm trying to make conversation here."

His words in no way made Chloe feel charitable. She held herself stiffly as she frowned at Gary. "I apologize, Professor Erickson. And yes, I'm enjoying the trip so far."

"Chloe, do you think you could cut the 'Professor Erickson' bit? We're both professionals, but we can also be a little more casual, don't you think? I'm not going to bite you."

Maybe he wouldn't bite, but would he rip her heart out again? That was a chance she couldn't take, and she had to keep her defenses up around him. She wasn't accustomed to his scathing remarks. She remembered how charming the old Gary could be when he wanted something. And he still had that irresistible appeal. She couldn't deny him anything when he looked at her the way he was looking now. Despite her reservations, she felt herself relax fractionally. "All right. As long as you don't accuse me of flirting anymore. I wish you could understand I have no interest in Brent. I've never heard such a ridiculous notion in my life."

Gary turned in his seat until he was facing Chloe. Chloe kept her face averted, though she could feel his curious stare.

She was glad to have her dark glasses to hide behind.

"Why is it so ridiculous? Don't you find Brent attractive?"

Chloe turned and gaped at Gary. "Brent? He's just a boy. A student where I teach. That's absurd."

"My guess is he's only a few years younger than you."

"So? I'm not remotely interested in him, or any man for that matter." *I could have still been interested in you, though,* she added to herself. Chloe crossed her arms over her chest in defense.

"What about that guy who drove you to the marina?" Gary persisted. "Didn't he say he's your fiancé?"

Chloe shifted uncomfortably. "Ex-fiancé. And how did we get on this topic, anyhow?"

"I guess it's my completely inept attempts at apologizing to you. Again. I'm sorry for the way I handled things. I just didn't like the way Brent was looking at you."

Time lapsed in silence as Chloe considered his words. Finally, he was apologizing for his behavior. Yet his reasoning for such behavior was peculiar. He didn't like how Brent looked at her? Why did he even care? Did this mean he was jealous of Brent? The idea was preposterous!

"Chloe? I was wondering something." Gary shifted in discomfort as she waited for him to continue. "Do you think we can start over? I've completely botched everything from the beginning of this excursion. I've said things to you I didn't mean. I've been harsh and unkind. Despite what you might think, I'm not usually like this. I don't know why I get crazy when I'm around you. Can you forgive me for being such an idiot?"

His plea caught her by surprise. She never expected him to admit the error of his ways, to say that he wanted a fresh start. He still hadn't mentioned breaking up with her six years ago, however. It was still as though their relationship had never existed. But at least he was apologizing for his recent behavior. He sounded vulnerable in a way Chloe never imagined possible for him. Would she forgive him? It would only set her up for more heartache. If he were anything like Trevor, he would sense weakness in her and use it to his advantage. She'd already seen how short-lived a man's apology could be.

"Yes, I'd like to start over, too," she found herself answering. Her sense of caution warred against the admission, yet Chloe knew it was right. She had to forgive him. She couldn't hold his mistakes against him.

"Thanks, Chloe. I'll do my best not to let you down again." Gary reached across the bench to give Chloe's hand a gentle squeeze.

Chloe gave him a tentative smile hoping she wouldn't regret meeting him halfway.

Once the tension was gone, Chloe and Gary were able to slip into easy conversation. Chloe was surprised to find how quickly the years seemed to slip away. They talked about people they used to know, music, television programs, sea turtles, and sunken ships. Neither of them brought up their relationship—Chloe was careful to steer clear of anything that might damage their comfortable rapport. The longer they talked, the more comfortable Chloe felt with Gary again. And the walls guarding her heart from him began to slip.

"How long have you studied Kemp's ridley turtles?" Chloe asked after several moments of easy silence had lapsed.

Gary shrugged. "Awhile. You know me. I've always been interested in the ocean. But I started studying the hawksbill. I still think they are the most beautiful of the sea turtles because of their unique shells."

"Jennifer said they are hunted for their shells."

"That's right," Gary answered. "There are a lot of poachers looking for hawksbill turtles. Their shells are beautiful and highly collectable, which makes for an endangered species. I've had a few run-ins with poachers. They're a rough lot. They don't understand why it's wrong to kill turtles when they have families to feed and buyers lining up for the shells."

"I guess I can understand their side—to a point," Chloe said after a moment. "Isn't there something those families can do to make money besides killing the turtles?"

"They cater to the tourists by selling little trinkets that don't bring in a lot of money. So they find what will make the greater cash quickly."

"Do you think we'll come across any poachers?" Chloe asked nervously.

"I doubt it. But don't worry. I know how to deal with them. Don't be afraid." He paused a moment, studying her. "When did you learn to dive?"

"When I was in college. I've always had a fascination with the ocean and what hides in the depths. When I was a kid I learned about the different pirate ships that sailed the Caribbean. I wanted to go there and find buried treasure."

"I imagine you spent a lot of time at the beach when you were a kid." He leaned back with a pleasant smile on his face.

Chloe shook her head. What Gary imagined was far from the truth. "Actually, my dad never wanted me to go to the beach. He said it represented a lazy lifestyle, and he wanted nothing to do with it." Chloe stiffened with the memories.

"Pretty harsh statement," Gary commented with a frown.

"I'm used to dealing with harsh men," she responded.

"And I haven't been any different, have I?" Gary asked with a self-deprecating smirk.

Chloe didn't answer. She didn't know what to say.

Unexpectedly, Gary took ahold of her hand and traced a pattern on her palm. He didn't seem to know what to say either. His touch created sensations that weren't altogether unpleasant. She didn't pull her hand out of his grasp.

"I'm glad you're here, Chloe—and not just to chaperone Jennifer. Although you're doing a great job with her. I can see many positive effects your influence is having on her."

Chloe wanted to hear about why he was really glad to have her on board, but she was curious to know what changes Jennifer had undergone. In a matter of a few days had Jennifer really changed for the better? "I haven't noticed any differences in her."

"A blind man would see the differences! She's smiling more, talking more, seems more confident. . . She's blossoming."

Chloe shook her head. Those weren't changes effected by her. Jennifer was responding to someone else, and it was a situation Chloe wished she could put an end to. Perhaps if Gary were aware, he would do something about it. "Gary, she's in love."

Gary looked stricken. Obviously the thought never occurred to him. "In love? With whom?"

Chloe wanted to groan with exasperation. The man could be so dense! If it didn't have anything to do with the ocean, Gary didn't pay attention. She was surprised he'd noticed any changes in Jennifer. Instead of berating him for having his head in the clouds, Chloe gently enlightened him. "She loves Brent. Can't you see the way her eyes light up whenever she looks at him? She adores him, and I'm afraid she's wasting her time."

Gary's eyes narrowed, and he looked at Chloe suspiciously. "And why would she be wasting her time? Is it because you have Brent's attention?"

Chloe flushed. Why did he persist in finding a connection between her and Brent? There was nothing between them! He had to stop being so ridiculously suspicious!

Brent was like an annoying little brother who needed discipline. He was a flirt with a cocky attitude and charming smile.

Unfortunately, Jennifer couldn't see that side of him.

"I know from personal experience what it's like to give your heart to someone who doesn't care!" Chloe retorted. "I don't want to see Jennifer pining after a guy who won't give her a second thought. It hurts too badly. And no matter what she does, she won't be able to get him to change his mind. Maybe he'll consider her for a short while, but she'll never meet his standards, and she'll only be disappointed—heartbroken—in the end. And God will have to rebuild that delicate trust and tattered hope ripped from her grasp.

"Am I the object of Brent's attention? I don't care! I only care about Jennifer." She stopped, out of breath and amazed she had shared so much.

Gary stared at her in surprise and consternation, and Chloe wondered if she had said too much. Seeing him again after so long had brought everything from the past bubbling to the surface. It had to be dealt with. The subject of their relationship had finally been broached. Chloe feared she had pushed too hard and too fast.

After an extended silence, through which Chloe held her breath in dread, Gary finally spoke. His words were devoid of emotion, and his gaze was shuttered. "Thanks for letting me know about this, Chloe. It's obvious you care deeply. I'll keep an eye on Brent and make sure he behaves honorably."

Chloe couldn't wait to escape Gary's presence. She was beginning to see that they couldn't move forward until they dealt with the past. It affected how they related to one another. They went up and down—arguing and apologizing. No matter how cool and professional they behaved, it was always there, looming over them. The thought of confronting Gary filled Chloe with trepidation. And there was nowhere she could run.

Forcing her thoughts from Gary, Chloe decided to log on

to the computer. The salon was empty, and she could check her E-mail account in private. She had only one E-mail from her mom. It was a nice, newsy letter that lifted Chloe's spirits. Her mom asked about the turtle research and told her about her father's mood swings. She didn't bring up Gary Erickson's name, for which Chloe was grateful. The note closed on disturbing news, however. Trevor was hanging around the house quite a bit in her absence.

Chloe wondered what Trevor was up to. Were he and her father plotting again? They could forget it! She knew her father still planned for her to marry Trevor. Unfortunately, he never took into consideration what God's will was for her. God wanted her to have a husband who would love her and lead her, as Christ loved the church. She couldn't imagine Trevor ever fulfilling that calling. If she were home, she would have Trevor to deal with. On the boat, she had to work with Gary. She wasn't sure which was more difficult.

❧

Chloe awoke with a start at 2:00 a.m. She wasn't sure what woke her; everything seemed quiet on the boat. She could hear the gentle lapping of the waves against the hull. She was about to fall back to sleep when she heard a strange sound. Someone was directly above her, pacing around the small galley.

Chloe waited for the person to stop so she could go back to sleep. He didn't stop. Chloe eased out of bed then changed into her shorts and T-shirt. Since she was wide-awake, she may as well investigate. Outside her room she paused, wondering if she should awaken Gary. But that was silly; it was probably Gary who was making the noise. Chloe silently crept up the stairway, peeking over the top stair. The salon and galley were dark and empty, but there was a light on in the pilothouse. Was it Uncle Howard? Chloe squinted, trying to see clearly in the dim light. It was useless. If it were her uncle, he would probably welcome her company. Yet if the person wasn't Uncle Howard, something was wrong. No one else had any business in the pilothouse at 2:00 a.m. Should she investigate, or go get her uncle? She paused in indecision.

"You're being silly, Chloe!" she reprimanded herself quietly. "Uncle Howard is most likely checking something on the boat, and you've turned it into a mystery."

Feeling braver and a little foolish, Chloe crept across the salon and galley to the pilothouse door. She paused just outside the door when she heard a voice speaking rapidly in Spanish.

"No, no tengo huevos de la tortuga todavía!"

It was Brent! Chloe wished she could interpret what he was saying, but she only knew a handful of Spanish words.

"Le prometo que tendra los huevos y el dinero pronto." Then there was silence.

Chloe moved forward, pressing her ear against the door. She was so intent on Brent's conversation, she didn't realize he'd stepped toward the doorway. He jerked the door open, grazing Chloe's cheek. Tears rushed to her eyes with the unexpected pain.

Chloe jumped back, clutching the side of her face while Brent glowered at her.

"What are you doing, Chloe?" he growled. His typically flirtatious manner was gone, and Chloe didn't recognize this side of Brent.

"I'm sorry, Brent. I didn't want to interrupt your conversation," she stammered. "I heard someone up here, and I came to investigate."

"You should have stayed in bed," he answered. Brent's eyes narrowed suspiciously. "How much did you overhear?"

Chloe shrugged. "It wouldn't matter if I heard the entire thing. I didn't understand a word of it. Whom were you talking to?"

Brent studied her for a moment as though weighing whether he could trust her. Suddenly his shoulders sagged, and he seemed to let down his guard. "It doesn't matter," he answered with a sigh. He took a step toward Chloe, pointing to her cheek. "You're hurt."

Chloe fingered her tender cheek. It throbbed where the door had smacked her. "It's not that bad."

"No, let me put some ice on it. Your cheek is beginning to swell." Brent slid the pilothouse door shut and stepped into the galley. He searched for a towel to hold the ice.

Dozens of questions darted through Chloe's mind as Brent remained silent. Who was he talking to? Why did the conversation take place at two in the morning and in Spanish? Why was he now edgy and suspicious of her?

"Here we go." Brent pressed a cold pack against Chloe's cheek. He rested one hand on her shoulder as he stared down at her.

She had to admit it did feel good against her throbbing face. But she didn't care for Brent's closeness. She took the pack from Brent and stepped back, shifting her gaze away from his. "I've got it, thanks."

Regardless of all the questions begging for answers, it was best to go back to her room. She didn't want to remain alone with Brent. She turned to leave, but Brent stopped her.

"Let's talk, Chloe. Come sit with me?"

Chloe hesitated. "I don't know. . . ." What did they have to talk about? Was he going to explain the conversation? She never felt comfortable with Brent, and it didn't seem like a good idea to be alone with him now.

"Just a few minutes," Brent pleaded. "I really want to talk with you." He wasn't teasing or flirting, his tone was completely serious. It piqued Chloe's curiosity.

Against her better judgment, she consented to Brent's

pleading. He led her into the salon and pointed her toward the sofa. The leather was cold when she sat tentatively at the far end of the sofa. Brent sat next to her—too close for her comfort.

"It's dark. Maybe we should turn on a light," she suggested. Light from the galley filtered into the salon, creating shadows across the room. Chloe felt edgy sitting in the darkened room with Brent. If Gary found them, it would renew his suspicions. Chloe shifted uncomfortably, wishing Brent would get to the point and let her go to her stateroom.

"What did you want to discuss, Brent?"

"I want to talk about you. Us. It isn't often that I get you alone."

"That's it? I thought you were going to tell me what's going on!" Chloe drew further away from Brent. "Didn't Professor Gary tell you not to pursue a relationship with me?"

Brent closed the space between them and rested his arm along the back of the sofa behind Chloe. He wound his fingers into Chloe's hair. "Who cares what Gary says? He's just jealous." Brent leaned closer as though he were planning to kiss her.

"Jealous?" Chloe laughed nervously as she inched further away. "Why would he be jealous? There's nothing between you and me."

"Nothing yet." Brent tried to kiss her. Chloe pushed him away and jumped to her feet.

"What are you thinking? There won't be anything between us! You need to go out with girls your own age who are interested in you."

Brent was clearly intrigued. "Are you saying you're not interested in me? Let's check just to be sure." He motioned for Chloe to return to her seat next to him. "Come on, Chloe."

Chloe shook her head and slowly backed away. "Listen,

Brent. I think I better go back to bed. I'm sorry I interrupted your conversation." As she turned to leave Brent jumped up and grabbed ahold of her hand, squeezing painfully.

"It was a mistake for you to hear that conversation. I don't care that you didn't understand it. You shouldn't have heard. You can't tell anyone about it—especially Gary."

Chloe stared at him in astonishment. It was amazing how quickly he could change demeanor. In one minute he was trying to kiss her, then he was menacing her.

"For your safety, Chloe, it would be best if you kept matters to yourself. You won't tell?"

It sounded like he'd just threatened her with physical harm. Was he dangerous? Or in danger? Chloe's mind raced. She wanted no part in his deception. She wouldn't lie to Gary if he asked her. If Brent was in danger, Gary should know immediately. The authorities had to be notified. He could be involved in anything she reasoned—drugs, smuggling, immigration, or any number of illegal activities. She should have stayed in bed. She didn't want to be a part of Brent's deception.

"Answer me!" Brent hissed. "Are you going to tell on me?"

Chloe opened her mouth to respond, but no sound came forth.

"What's going on up here?" Gary boomed from the top of the stairs. He flipped on a lamp. Bright light illumined the salon. Chloe squinted and pulled her hand from Brent's grasp.

"What are you two doing up here?" Gary demanded.

Chloe dropped her gaze, unable to face Gary's scowl. "Nothing's going on. I was just going back to bed," she stammered. She wanted to tell Gary about Brent's conversation in order to clear herself. She cast a glance a Brent who stared defiantly at Gary. There was no way she could expose him. She had no idea what he was involved in. She only hoped he wouldn't say anything to make matters worse.

Gary glared at the pair of them. "It doesn't look like 'nothing.' Tell me why I've caught the two of you sitting in the dark, alone, in the middle of the night."

Brent didn't answer, but his posture relaxed. He confidently crossed his arms over his chest and threw Chloe a cheeky wink.

It was the worst thing he could do to support her innocence.

Gary scowled, his mind obviously made up. "What am I supposed to do about you two? Chloe, you're supposed to be a professional! I can't have you making clandestine meetings in the middle of the night with one of my students. I ask you again, what was going on?"

Chloe winced, appalled by the situation. Once again, Gary had wrongly accused her, and his mind was set by his so-called evidence. "You wouldn't believe me if I told you." Frustration laced her words. She wouldn't let Gary know how much his distrust wounded her. Rather than try to explain, Chloe moved away from Brent and headed toward the stairs. Gary let her pass then followed her below. Chloe knew he was behind her—shadowing her like an angry jailer. She wondered what his sentence would be this time. She hadn't deliberately sought out Brent, but that would be impossible to explain. The circumstances spoke too loudly for any sound explanation. She turned at her door, wanting to clear her name—however unlikely that would be.

She looked up at Gary and winced at the fierce look he gave her. "It's not what it looks like, Gary. I heard someone upstairs and went to investigate. I didn't know it was Brent. I didn't know who—"

"Does it really matter what happened up there?" His voice was gravelly with emotion.

"Yes, it does! I wasn't—"

Gary pressed his finger to Chloe's lips. "Don't say any more."

Chloe backed away, insistent on explaining herself. "But I need to make this clear. You have to understand that Brent and I—"

"No. I believe you." And before Chloe could say another word, Gary pulled her against his chest and pressed his lips to hers in a firm kiss. The kiss became tender as it deepened. Then it was over, leaving Chloe to wonder how it possibly happened.

Gary pulled away, looking as stunned as Chloe felt. "Go back to bed, Chloe," he said in a voice that didn't sound like his.

Chloe did as she was instructed, feeling as though she were already dreaming.

❧

The next morning Chloe wasn't sure how to face Gary. How did he feel about her and what had that brief kiss meant to him? Dozens of possibilities raced through her mind. She wondered if Brent had been right about Gary feeling jealous. Or maybe it had been the only way he could think of to get her to stop talking at two o'clock in the morning. Possibly, in the worst-case scenario, Gary thought that she was the kind of girl who would accept kisses from any willing guy. If he believed she kissed anyone who came along, then she didn't know how she could ever face him again. And what would she say if he wanted to talk about it?

Her worries were unfounded, because Gary didn't even look at her when she stepped into the galley. He and Brent were sitting in silence as they ate frozen waffles warmed in the toaster. Jennifer was nowhere to be found, which disappointed Chloe. She could use Jennifer's presence to help buffer these two men. She didn't want to deal with either one.

Very quietly, so as not to draw attention from the two men, Chloe selected a fresh grapefruit and took her breakfast out to the aft deck. It was a beautiful morning, and they were anchored near Puerto el Mezquital. It was another small town. Uncle Howard preferred to anchor in the bay rather than search for a place to dock late at night. Though the town seemed unimpressive, the coastline was lush and green. Off in the distance Chloe could see the seagulls diving for small fish in the warm waves. It's paradise, Chloe reflected. If only she could get her thoughts off last night.

Uncle Howard joined her on the deck. He pulled out the chair next to Chloe and sat with a contented sigh. "Beautiful morning."

Chloe barely responded.

"What's going on in that head of yours, Chloe-girl?" he asked with concern.

Chloe shrugged. She wanted to talk about it, and she knew she could trust her uncle, but where to start? "How did you sleep last night?" she asked as she cut open her grapefruit and scooped out a bite of the juicy, pink pulp.

Uncle Howard stared intently at Chloe's somber expression. "Better than you, is my guess. Something happened?"

Chloe nodded and poured the story out to her uncle— everything from her concerns over Brent's mysterious behavior to Gary's unexpected kiss. "I never expected him to kiss me, and I still don't understand why he did it."

Howard chuckled. "I'm not surprised it happened. Not at all. When you two are in the same room together, sparks fly."

Chloe shook her head at her uncle's ridiculous implication. "You think we're still attracted to each other? I'm not so sure. Too much has happened. If we could just keep things friendly—"

"He professes to be a Christian?" Howard asked.

"Yes, but—"

"And you just said you find him attractive."

"I did? Well, sure. But the thing is—"

"Quit worrying about it, Chloe! It'll all come together." Howard leaned back with a satisfied smile. "You trust God to work out the kinks. I like the professor—he's grown into a fine man. He's energetic. Reminds me of myself at that age. Why are you looking at me like that?" Howard demanded.

Chloe laughed in disbelief. "You think Gary resembles you? That's impossible! He's gruff and grumpy. He isn't happy-go-lucky like you. You and Gary are nothing alike. I'm sorry, Uncle Howard, but I just don't see it."

"And you think what you see is accurate?" Howard's voice was clearly skeptical. "Forgive me for being blunt with you, Chloe-girl, but you measure every man by your father. If he has a trait similar to what you see in your ol' dad, you peg him for a loser and run like mad."

Chloe set her spoon down and stared at her uncle. "That's not true! I don't compare men to my dad. I'm just cautious and for good reason, wouldn't you say?"

Uncle Howard leaned back in his chair and crossed his arms over his chest. "Cautious is good, yes, but you are afraid. Now don't glare at me. I'm just saying it as I see it. You're afraid of getting hurt—of ending up with someone who won't value you. I can understand that. But if you never take a chance, you'll never experience the good things in life. God gives us many things, but He never forces us to take them. That's our decision. Are you going to receive or not?"

It was a good question—one that Chloe didn't have an answer for. Had God brought her and Gary together to repair the damage from the past? Her mind balked at the idea, but her heart was intrigued. "I need to think about it," she answered finally with a sigh.

"Just so you don't think too long and the opportunity passes you by. You'll always regret the one that got away." His attitude allowed no room for a rebuttal. "Now, I'm going to talk to

Brent about what he was doing in the pilothouse last night. He has no business being in there." He stood, but Chloe grabbed ahold of his hand.

"Please don't mention anything to Brent. If you speak to him, he'll know I told you. I don't want to make matters worse." Chloe remembered the desperate look on Brent's face. Whatever he was involved in, it wasn't good.

Uncle Howard didn't look pleased, but he consented. "Then you and I have to keep our ears open. You see anything else suspicious, you come get me. Maybe I can catch him in the act myself; then you won't be in the middle."

The sliding door opened, bringing the conversation to an abrupt end. Jennifer joined them at the table. She seemed bright and cheerful, and hopefully oblivious to last night's episode.

"I hope you're in a good mood," she greeted as she set her cereal bowl on the table and pulled up a matching chair. "Those men inside are a grumpy lot. Did something happen? Hey, what happened to your cheek, Chloe?"

Chloe shifted uncomfortably. Her cheek was no longer swollen from where the door hit her, but it looked like she slept on a sandpaper pillow. "It's nothing, really. Just a little mishap. Did you sleep well?"

Jennifer took a bite of her cereal. "I always do on a boat. Rocks me to sleep like a baby. And this is a really nice boat," she added, casting a smile at Howard.

Chloe sighed with relief, glad she didn't have to explain what happened in the night. She wished Jennifer didn't have her heart set on Brent. He wasn't the right man for her. Chloe wanted to warn Jennifer to stay away from him, that he couldn't be trusted. Yet she wasn't in a position to say anything. She hoped Gary had again warned Brent to keep to himself.

"Look at that, Chloe!" Jennifer exclaimed, pointing toward

the beach many yards away. She jumped up from her seat and ran to the rail. "Come look! It's a big one!"

Chloe stared at the sandy shore, trying to see what drew Jennifer's attention. Finally she spotted a large sea turtle. It seemed to be basking in the early sunlight. "Is it nesting?" she asked.

Jennifer shrugged. "I'm not an expert on turtle behavior, but it looks like the turtle is stranded. I think it's a loggerhead sea turtle. See how large the shell is and how thick it is through the neck? They usually nest at night."

Chloe frowned. "If it isn't nesting then something must be wrong with it. Am I correct? If we don't do anything, will the turtle die on the beach?" Without waiting for an answer Chloe grabbed a pair of binoculars from behind the outdoor bar and rejoined Jennifer at the railing. It took a moment for her to fix her gaze steadily on the turtle. When she finally brought him into focus, she gasped at the sight of him. "Jennifer! He doesn't have any flippers on his left side! And look at all the fishing line tangled around him!"

Jennifer grabbed the binoculars from Chloe for a look. "Oh, no! I don't know how he's stayed alive. He doesn't look too good."

"Do you think it was a shark that got his fins?"

Jennifer nodded as she continued to study the turtle through the binoculars. "Probably. We need to get him back in the water."

"What should we do? We have to tell Gary." Chloe took a step backward and bumped into someone.

"At your service," Gary quipped. He steadied Chloe, looking past her toward the beach. "What do we have here?" He took the binoculars from Jennifer and studied the turtle for a matter of seconds. "Who wants to go with me to check him?" he asked.

Hasty arrangements were made to rescue the turtle. Uncle Howard lowered the dinghy into the water. Gary, Jennifer, and Chloe hopped into the motor-powered raft and quickly buzzed the short distance to the beach. The sea turtle hadn't moved, and Chloe wondered if it was still alive. Once they reached shallow waters, Gary jumped out and pulled the dinghy up to the beach.

Chloe and Jennifer ran over to the turtle as soon as they could jump out of the raft. It was an enormous animal! Gary knelt with them and assessed the loggerhead's situation. The turtle began flapping his good fins, trying desperately to get away.

"He's making it worse! The fishing line is wrapped around his neck now!" Chloe exclaimed.

Gary nodded. "We need to cut it off him. He's handicapped as it is without being tangled. Look—his front fin is chewed up and the rear one was completely torn off."

"How can we help?" Chloe asked as she watched Gary pull the tangled line from the turtle's fins. She didn't have a knife or scissors, and all Gary had was a small pocketknife.

"Here. . .help me get it from around his neck. Jennifer, try to clear the rear flipper," Gary grunted as he tried to free the turtle's head. The turtle didn't appreciate the ministrations and tried to snap at Gary's hand. "Watch his mouth! He's stressed."

Gary's warning came too late. When Chloe reached for the turtle's head to help with the fishing line the turtle clamped down hard, grazing her forearm. The sharp bill sliced into her tender flesh. "Aah!"

"Chloe!" Gary grabbed ahold of her arm. It was difficult to tell how deep the cut was because of the profuse bleeding. Gary pulled off his shirt and wrapped it around Chloe's arm. "I'm sorry! That was my fault! Can you hang on a minute longer?

We almost have the turtle free."

"I'm okay. Just get him back in the water," Chloe answered. Her arm burned, but she didn't think the turtle did too much damage. She sat back in the sand and watched Jennifer and Gary free the turtle in record time.

"We're going to have to drag him into the water, and he's a heavy one!" Gary groaned. He and Jennifer gripped the turtle's thick shell by his hindquarters and pulled him the two feet into the water. Gary steered him into knee-deep waves. Chloe held her breath. The turtle wasn't responding. Then, with a quick slap of its good fins, the loggerhead paddled away.

Gary flashed Chloe a triumphant grin. "He's going to be okay!" He lumbered up the beach to where Chloe was sitting, his shirt still wrapped around her arm. Blood had soaked through. Gary's smile faded into a frown. "Let's get you back to the boat and take care of your arm. I hope you won't need stitches, because I have no idea where the nearest hospital is."

"It's not that bad, Gary. Just a little nick," Chloe answered. She tried to stand but felt light-headed. Gary caught her and held her steady. With one arm around her waist, he guided her to the raft and helped her into it. They waited while Jennifer gathered all the fishing line that had entangled the loggerhead.

Back on The Bounty Chloe received more attention than she would have liked. Brent raced for the first aid kit, her uncle carefully cleaned her wound, and Gary prepared to bandage it.

"I'm fine, really!" she insisted, but no one seemed to hear. The wound was just a little nick and wouldn't need stitches. It certainly didn't warrant so much attention.

"I'll take over," Gary declared once Uncle Howard finished

cleaning the injury. Uncle Howard and Brent left the galley, leaving Gary and Chloe alone.

"It's just a little cut. Nothing to worry about," she muttered for what seemed the hundredth time.

"We'll see," Gary answered grimly. He took a thick gauze bandage from the first aid kit and pressed it to Chloe's arm. He then wrapped more gauze around her arm to hold the bandage in place.

"Gary, you're mummifying my arm," Chloe complained as he continued to wind the bandage. He had the gauze covering the entire area from her wrist up to her elbow. The superficial bite was only two inches long in the middle of her arm.

"Can't be too cautious," he muttered as he added a second layer of gauze. "Are you feeling light-headed still?"

Chloe shook her head. "No. I'm fine. And will you stop!" She stilled his hands by grabbing the gauze.

Gary reluctantly cut the gauze and secured the end of the bandage. "I shouldn't have been so careless. It was my fault that turtle bit you. I was in such a hurry to get him free."

"It wasn't your fault. And I'm okay. Just a little bite, okay?" She watched him, wishing she could remove the worry from his eyes. She was warmed by it, nevertheless.

"It could have been much worse." He gazed at her, his expression troubled. "I never wanted to hurt you."

"You didn't hurt me. It was just an accident."

"Chloe, I—I'm not just talking about the turtle. I've been trying to find a way to tell you—"

"We just saw your loggerhead surface by the boat!" Brent said as he burst into the room.

A pained expression crossed Gary's face, and Chloe sighed in exasperation. It seemed they never caught a break. There had been so many misunderstandings and so little time to really talk.

"Is he still out there?" Gary asked impatiently. The question was directed at Brent, but Gary didn't take his gaze from Chloe's face.

"Yeah! And he keeps turning upside down. You should go see!"

Reluctantly Gary turned from Chloe. "We'll finish this later," he promised then went out to see the floundering loggerhead.

Brent was quick to take the place Gary evacuated. He moved in close so Chloe felt trapped in the small galley. She ignored him by busying herself with packing the first aid supplies.

"Is there something going on between you and the professor, Chloe?" Brent asked.

Chloe sucked in her breath. Was it that obvious? Sure, she was still attracted to Gary, but she didn't think anyone else had noticed. If Brent had picked up on it and her uncle knew, then Gary would be aware, too. This could become humiliating if she wasn't more careful with her feelings. "Whatever gave you that idea?" she asked casually. Inside her heart started thumping.

"I see the way you look at each other. And he's told me plenty of times to stay away from you. I just figured you two have something going on."

She didn't want to have this conversation—and definitely not with Brent, of all people. He didn't know about the kiss or their previous relationship. Brent would have said something. But it was enough that he suspected attraction between her and Gary. She didn't want to discuss it when she didn't understand it herself. "He's my boss for this trip and a colleague."

Brent didn't look convinced. "Well, in that case, I still have a chance. I was a little worried you were hung up on the professor. But now I still have time to convince you I'm not such a bad guy. I'll make you forget all about the professor."

"I think we should go out on deck with everyone else, Brent. I'd like to see the turtle, too," Chloe insisted.

"Oh, I just made that up. We saw the turtle surface, but then he swam away just fine. I needed an excuse to get the professor outside so I could talk to you. He hangs around you too much."

"You lied about the turtle just to spend time with me?" Chloe gave him a cold look, hoping he would leave her alone and forget any interest he might have in her. She didn't want his attention, and she didn't need any more probing questions. Imagine playing such childish games! "I'm going outside, too," she said as she brushed past Brent.

Brent grabbed ahold of her hand with his firm grasp. "You haven't told the professor about my little midnight conversation, have you?"

She had told her uncle, but she could honestly answer Brent. "No, I haven't told Gary." She quickly hurried away before Brent could question her further.

Chloe joined the others on the deck. Gary had found another turtle. He was lying on his belly on the swim deck with a juvenile green sea turtle scuttling about in front of him.

Chloe joined him, sitting cross-legged on the deck. "Where did this little guy come from?" she asked, already forgetting her conversation with Brent as she watched Gary rub the turtle's shell.

"I actually caught him," Gary said sheepishly. "I came out here to see the loggerhead, but this guy was swimming by instead. I scooped him up with your uncle's fishing net."

Chloe watched in fascination as the turtle became passive under Gary's gentle touch.

"They're very sensitive creatures," he explained. "Despite what most people think, turtles can feel someone touching their shell, and it gives them pleasure. It's like petting a dog or cat."

"Can I try it?" Chloe asked, moving closer. Chloe reached past him and rubbed the turtle's brown and green shell. She could feel all the pock and dent marks, but the shell was cool and smooth. She was amazed that the turtle could feel her rubbing through the hard shell.

"Chloe, about last night. . ." Gary hesitated.

Chloe stiffened. He was going to talk about the kiss. She looked up to find Brent watching them with interest. She knew he would hang on every word. Brent had no business hearing about the kiss. She just wanted to forget the entire night ever happened.

"Let's just forget about it," she whispered so Brent couldn't hear. "I'm sure you were going to say it was a big mistake, so let me say it for you. It was a mistake. We won't give it another thought." She passed one hand over her hair, tucking the loose strands behind her ear. There, it was said. She saved Gary from having to embarrass her. But was that what he really meant to say? At the stricken look on Gary's face, she realized she might have it all wrong. How did he really feel about the kiss?

Gary frowned at her, a crease forming between his brows. "That's not what I was going to say. But if that's how you feel, then we won't speak of it again." Dropping his gaze from her face, he smoothed his features until all expression was gone. Once again he was completely professional. Chloe wasn't sure she liked the transformation. "I'll have some more notes for you to type up tonight. Also, I'll need you to catalog this turtle's information once we get him tagged."

She found Brent staring at her in triumph. A lump formed in her throat as she realized how much she'd messed up.

After their conversation, Chloe noticed a definite cooling in Gary's attitude toward her. He didn't go so far as to call her Miss Crenshaw, but she knew he wished they weren't together on the same boat. Chloe felt terrible. She had spoken too soon in an effort to protect herself from being humiliated. Now Gary was angry with her, and she didn't blame him. She knew she could let it go and hope he would forget about it. They could continue with a professional and impersonal relationship for the rest of the trip. But Chloe couldn't live with that. She couldn't accept that she had hurt someone and not try to rectify it. She hurried into the salon to write Gary a note of apology.

> *Dear Gary,*
> *I didn't mean to make you feel bad. I was just protecting myself. I couldn't face rejection again, so I guess I rejected you first. I'm sorry. I'm so sorry. Can we have another new beginning? Friends?*
>
> > *Yours,*
> > *Chloe*

She added it to the stack of notes she worked on that evening and left them by the computer for Gary. She hoped he would read over the notes like he did every night. Then he would get her message and understand.

Chloe waited all evening for a response, worried that her note had fallen into the wrong hands and wishing she had e-mailed him instead. Gary continued to avoid her and was irritable with anyone who tried to talk to him. Finally, Chloe gave up and went to her cabin. It was obvious to her that Gary was through playing games. The rejection stung, but she figured she deserved it. She had made one too many mistakes.

It was late that night after Chloe had gone to bed when a note was pressed under her door. At the sound, Chloe's heart began to beat in a rapid tempo of hope. "Please, Lord, let him forgive me," she whispered.

She turned on the bedside light and slipped from the bed. The note brought a sigh of relief to her lips. It was only one word, but it meant everything.

Friends

five

Chloe? How would you feel about going diving?" Brent asked a few days later. "Professor Gary and Howard have decided we'll stay here an extra day. Storms are in the forecast, and we'll want to see as much as we can before the water gets churned up. Everything goes into hiding when a storm blows through."

Reluctantly, Chloe saved the notes she had been working on for Gary. It seemed whenever she got to the end of one set of dictation, he would hand her a new one. "All right, Brent. I'm coming. Just give me a minute to get changed."

"Don't take too long." Brent grimaced. "We don't have all day."

Once in her suit she rushed out to the back deck where Gary and Brent were waiting for her. Like last time, Jennifer helped Chloe get her air tank and mask on. Gary waited wordlessly as he watched her fumble with hurried fingers.

"Ready?" he asked.

Chloe nodded, placing the regulator in her mouth. She followed Brent and Gary into the water. They swam ahead of her and at a fast pace.

Gary motioned excitedly toward a mound of rocks. As Chloe drew closer it seemed as though the rocks were moving with the current. Dozens upon dozens of corals waved in the water, being pulled back and forth. Tiny, colorful fish darted in and out of the crevices. Chloe tried to see what Gary was particularly excited about. She swam closer, careful not to bump into him. He pointed into one of the larger crevices.

Inside were two juvenile green sea turtles. Their shells were about the size of a cantaloupe. Gary grinned at her around his regulator, sending up tiny bubbles.

Brent pressed past Chloe and Gary then reached into the crevice to grab one of the young turtles. Gary shook his head vigorously, but Brent ignored him. Chloe wanted to scold Brent for disturbing the turtles. It was obvious they were already frightened since they retreated into the rocks for safety. He had made it worse by antagonizing them.

A shock of bubbles went up from Brent when he jerked his arm out of the crevice. One of the turtles had bit his fingertip, and now he was bleeding in the water.

Serves him right for sticking his hand in a dark hole, Chloe mused. Thankfully, he'd only been nicked by the turtle's sharp mouth.

Gary pointed toward the surface, urging Brent to go up. There were a few sharks circling the reef, and sharks were always interested in blood. Brent heeded Gary and retreated to the boat above them.

Once Brent was gone, Chloe didn't feel any particular urgency to end her underwater exploration. Maybe they would see some more turtles or an ancient shipwreck. Gary motioned for her to follow him. Chloe turned in the water, but something caught her eye, and she paused. It was a huge shell, and it was moving. She looked closely at the rocks, wondering if it had been a figment of her imagination. But no, wait. There it was again—a shell almost as big as her head, and it was moving.

Chloe moved in closer, realizing it was a giant hermit crab. It was the biggest hermit crab she had ever seen! She reached toward the crab, more cautiously than Brent had. She exhaled, causing herself to sink closer to the rocks. I'd like to see how heavy it is.

When a long, sleek fish bumped her, Chloe realized something was wrong. Shark! And not just one but several. Black tip reef sharks—and they were darting about aggressively. They weren't very big, only about three feet long, but that was plenty big for Chloe. She didn't mind watching them on TV as they slashed through the water near coral reefs. Swimming with them was a different story. And they obviously didn't like her intrusion. Chloe froze, unsure what to do. She knew the sharks didn't consider her their natural enemy, yet she felt a tremor of uncertainty. More sharks were coming. She watched in amazement as one particularly large shark swam near her then snatched a reef fish with its strong jaws. He thrashed about, drawing more sharks to him. Chloe felt the stirring in the water caused by the shark's flailing.

She stiffened when she felt something brush against her waist. Another shark? Relief flooded her when she realized it was Gary. He gripped her waist and slowly drew her away from the reef and away from the sharks. They swam toward the surface, the hermit crab she had been so curious about all but forgotten.

Brent was waiting for them on the back dive platform along with Uncle Howard and Jennifer. Uncle Howard pulled Chloe out of the water.

"You should have seen all the sharks down there." Chloe shivered at the thought. It had been a little too close for her comfort. "Why did they gather like that?" she asked Gary as he pulled himself onto the platform.

"Probably the scent of a fresh kill," Gary said as he pulled off his mask and shrugged off the air tank. "Did you see how that one went after the fish?"

Chloe shuddered. Yes, she had seen. It happened only a few feet in front of her.

Howard stood, towering over everyone. "Storm's brewing.

We need to get everything secured now, folks." He strode to the salon door with Brent and Jennifer following obediently.

Chloe found herself alone with Gary on the aft deck. Her gaze locked on his, and she forgot about how wet she was and that she needed to help the others. Gary gazed at her evenly, and Chloe wondered what he was thinking.

Gary took a small step toward her. "There's so much I want to say to you. I'm afraid that if I don't hurry up and say it, someone will interrupt, and I'll miss my chance. Chloe, I know I haven't always done or said the right thing. But do you think you could ever trust me again?"

Chloe shifted uncomfortably, averting her gaze from his steady one. She clasped her hands tightly in front of her. "Trust? I think that's a little difficult for both of us, don't you agree? It's the source of all our problems. I wish. . ." She faltered, unsure how to continue under Gary's watchful eyes.

"You wish what?" he pressed.

"I wish I knew how everything would work out. I wish I had known before." She couldn't help the rush of tears that came to her eyes. Embarrassment made her look away so Gary wouldn't see how vulnerable she was.

The wind was picking up speed, making the waves choppier. The boat rocked heavily. Chloe swayed. Balancing on the deck suddenly took all her attention. Gary gripped her arm and held her gently.

"The storm is coming." He didn't seem concerned.

Chloe wished she felt so calm. Her stomach churned as the boat rocked and lurched on the waves. The combination of the storm and Gary's touch made her uneasy. "You don't seem worried," she whispered.

Gary shrugged. "There's nothing to worry about—unless you get seasick easily. Then we may have a problem." He took a step closer to Chloe. "Do you really think it was a mistake?"

Chloe knew he was referring to the kiss. Color crept into her cheeks. "I'm not sure. I know I didn't handle it well when you wanted to talk about it. I just didn't want to discuss it in front of Brent."

Gary nodded. "And that was my mistake. I never should have brought it up without making sure no one else was around. Can we start over—again?" He took another step toward her. "We could give it another try and find out if. . ."

"If it was a mistake?" she asked, only to fill the charged silence.

Gary nodded, staring at her mouth.

The boat lurched, and Chloe swayed toward Gary. She fit comfortably in his arms—as she always had. Just as he was about to kiss her, Chloe pictured Trevor Renolds. The memory of his sneer caused her to stiffen. He told her she'd never appeal to a man as she was. She wasn't very attractive—disappointing. Chloe caught her bottom lip between her teeth. Gary had never said those awful things to her, but he was the one who'd left her for another woman. No! She couldn't let him kiss her again. Six years of pain was too much to risk suffering once more. She couldn't hazard getting close again.

She pulled her arm away from Gary's grasp. "I'm sorry. I can't!" She turned and fled to the safety of her stateroom.

❧

Down in her stateroom, Chloe changed into warm sweatpants and a T-shirt. The boat was rocking more violently than she thought possible without capsizing. It was difficult to stand without being thrown against the wall or across the bed. Several times she lost her footing. Sweat broke out across her forehead as she considered the possibilities of danger. She knew the waves were high and choppy. They easily tossed The Bounty as though it were a child's toy. What if the boat did capsize? She could swim well enough to scuba dive. Swimming in a raging storm was a completely different matter. In the bathroom her makeup bag slid off the counter and crashed to the floor. Tiny tubes and bottles rolled in all directions. Chloe closed her eyes, wishing the storm to end. Nervous nausea churned in her stomach. "Please, God, don't let us die like this. Help me to be brave. I don't think I can stand it a minute longer."

She slowly sank to the floor, willing her stomach to return to normal. Fear pulsed in her mind, creating an ache in her temples. She had to get off the boat! A firm tap sounded at her door. "Chloe? Are you all right?"

Gary! With effort, Chloe rose and crossed the swaying room to the door. Somehow she was able to stay on her feet and pry the door open.

"Chloe!"

Somehow Gary knew just what she needed. He stepped into the room and pulled her into his arms. She gleaned strength from his embrace as he held her. The storm continued to toss the boat, but now it didn't matter. She knew she would be safe with Gary.

"How did you know?" she murmured against his shoulder. "How did you know I was scared?"

Gary shifted and looked down at her. "I remember how upset you used to become over storms. You've always been scared of strong wind and heavy rain. I couldn't let you sit in here and brave the storm alone. On the plus side, your uncle said this should be a quick storm. It'll be over before you know it."

"The boat is okay?" Visions of sinking in the tumultuous waves filled Chloe's mind again, and she shivered involuntarily.

Gary's nod was confident. "The boat is fine. Everyone upstairs is fine. Your uncle is positive we're going to get through this quickly without damage. Besides, Chloe, you can't forget that God protects you. He watches over you and doesn't want any harm to come your way. You'll be safe in His care. We're both safe."

Chloe sagged against Gary, thankful for his comfort. He seemed to know exactly what she needed to hear. She felt better having him near, but the fear hadn't abated completely. It probably wouldn't disappear until the storm was over.

Gary brushed his finger down her cheek. "Stop worrying. Why don't we talk about something else to take your mind off the storm?"

"Like what?" she whispered. The boat lurched, and she sucked in her breath. "Where are the life jackets?"

Gary ignored her question. "Do you want to tell me why you ran away from me earlier?" he asked instead.

Chloe thought about the way he almost kissed her again and shook her head. Explaining her fears to Gary was as bad as facing the storm. She wasn't sure she could do either.

Gary didn't accept her silence. "Is it me? Would you like me to leave you alone? I don't mean to force myself at you."

"I just feel confused when I'm around you. It's as though time has taken a backward turn. I'm just not sure I can risk going back."

"It's all about trust, isn't it?" Gary asked. He tucked a stray wisp of hair behind Chloe's ear.

Chloe shrugged. "That's putting it simply. I'm just not certain I am capable of those feelings any longer."

"Why don't you sit?" Gary suggested, pointing toward the bed. He remained near the open door. "I need to tell you something. I should have shared this with you long ago, but I never had the courage to do it."

Chloe held her breath, uncertain whether she wanted to know or not. She was suddenly aware of every inflection in Gary's voice and every emotion that flickered in his eyes.

Clearly this wasn't easy for him. "You don't have to tell me if you don't want to," she offered.

Gary took a deep breath. "I have to tell you." He paused before continuing. "Do you remember the woman I told you about when we broke up?"

Chloe nodded. How could I forget? Those moments had forever changed her life. Even now she could remember the humiliation she had felt.

"There was no woman."

Chloe gasped incredulously. Had she heard him correctly? "What—are—you saying?" she ground out between clenched teeth.

Gary's laugh was self-deprecating. "There wasn't a woman. I lied to you. I felt I had no choice." When Chloe tried to interrupt, Gary held up his hand. "No, let me finish. I have to explain. Then you can lash out at me as I well deserve."

Chloe lapsed into an uneasy silence, waiting for Gary to continue.

"I was twenty-two years old, almost finished with college, and I was in debt up to my eyeballs. I had this beautiful, wonderful girlfriend who had stars in her eyes every time she looked at me. And that scared me. Don't think I didn't love you, because I did—more than I ever thought possible. But in this case love just wasn't enough. Love wouldn't pay my student loans. Love wouldn't get me a job that would support us—much less make your father like me. I knew you wanted to take things one day at a time, but all I could see was the future, and it was frightening.

"I had a wonderful opportunity once I finished college. I hired on to be the marine consultant for a new oil drilling in the South Atlantic. It was a two-year commitment, and it paid well. But one of the stipulations was that I had to be single. They didn't want family complications on such a remote expedition. It was an incredible opportunity. Most marine biologists fresh out of college have to wait tables to earn a living. I couldn't turn it down.

"I planned to pay off all my student loans and save some money. And when the two years were over I hoped to come home to you and beg your forgiveness. It seemed like a good plan at the time. But breaking up with you was the hard part. I loved you too much to just call it quits. I thought if I made you furious it would be easier for you to handle. That's why I told you there was another woman. I wish I could do it all over again—make it right this time. I'm sorry, Chloe."

As Gary lapsed into silence, Chloe struggled to digest all he had told her. There was never another woman! It was a small comfort next to all the suffering she'd endured. He lied to her! He lied just so he could be free to gallivant around the globe! Night after night she had cried herself to sleep, wondering where she had gone wrong. How dare he? And why bother telling her now—after six long years of separation? It only served to renew the pain she thought was long buried.

"Get out! Get out, Gary! I wish I never had to see you again!"

Wordlessly, Gary left. Chloe threw herself back on her bed to shed fresh tears of anguish and betrayal.

❧

The storm finally ended, though Chloe didn't pay much heed. The pounding rain and riotous waves were gone. The sunshine came back, peeking through the clouds. Listlessly, she left her stateroom—feeling spent from crying her heart out.

Howard stepped in from the pilothouse. "Storm's over, folks, and you should see the rainbow!"

Everyone but Chloe hurried outside. She wandered over to the computer and logged on to her E-mail account. The message waiting for her brought a pounding to her temple.

It was from Trevor. After all Gary had told her, the last thing she wanted was to hear from Trevor. Her stomach turned as she opened the message. She wondered how Trevor got her E-mail. He must have gotten it from her father.

Chloe,

I'm surprised I haven't heard from you in these weeks. You have my E-mail address. I imagine you've been busy chasing turtles. I've spent most of my spare time visiting with your parents, especially your father. He feels confident that you and I can work out our relationship. He thinks you're being stubborn, but I wonder if you're not just afraid. You don't have to be afraid of our future together. I'll take good care of you and make sure your life is perfect. If you'll only come home! I've been following your excursion. I can't say I understand the importance of it. Please consider coming home early. I'm eagerly waiting for you.

Your fiancé,
Trevor

Chloe groaned inwardly. Of course Trevor didn't understand the importance of the trip. He never took time to consider anything that was important to her. He still didn't get it. She didn't want to marry him! It would be better to remain single and avoid all these difficult entanglements.

"Lord, I pray You'll help me. I feel so betrayed by Gary." Fresh tears rushed to her eyes. She squeezed her eyes shut to keep them from falling. "I don't want to hurt anymore, and I don't want to think about Trevor. I pray You'll help me work all this out before I lose my mind!" It wasn't a classic prayer, but it did much to bring peace to Chloe's troubled heart.

She was about to join the others out on deck when Howard came stomping in from the pilothouse. He didn't look happy.

"What is it? Has something happened?"

Howard gave her a grim nod. "We're stuck here. It looks like the wiring is shot. My number two engine won't start."

Chloe hurried after him. "Is it something you can fix?" They were about ten miles offshore, and Chloe had no idea where the nearest town was. What if they didn't have the necessary boat parts? They would be stuck in Mexico until something could be done.

Chloe followed him down into the engine room. Everything looked normal to her, but Howard was glowering. He jerked open a door where colored wires intermingled and twisted in all directions. He muttered angrily under his breath.

"Can you see anything wrong?" she asked.

Howard nodded. "We need to be towed to the nearest town."

six

Where are we going?" Chloe asked Gary as they walked down the dirt road past the marina. They were back to being cautiously professional with each other. Chloe didn't want to talk about the past or consider a future with Gary. It was easier to just be the secretary and chaperone and hope the trip ended soon so she could get on with her life. Once she got home, she planned to look for a new job—one far away from Professor Gary Erickson!

They were in the business district of the town Punta de Piedra—if you could call it a town. Village seemed a more appropriate word. There were a few people in the shops; most loitered in the doorways. Chloe took out her camera and snapped a few pictures of the authentic Mexico that few tourists see. She knew some of the people were tourists—they were distinctly American with cameras in hand and confused expressions. Chloe was sure she wore the same expression when hawkers approached her, asking her to buy. Some of the hawkers were just children trying to sell their trinkets. Peddlers with pushcarts shoved necklaces in Chloe's face, saying, "Almost free!" Shop owners called to them from the doorways.

Chloe was glad when they finally reached the last shop on the strip. No one followed them as they continued to walk along the dirt road. Chloe noticed there were few buildings lining the dirt road ahead. None of them promised to be prosperous businesses. Most were run-down homes no larger than the size of a shed. Chickens squawked in the yards.

Clothes hung on lines, flapping in the gentle breeze. Stray dogs barked and chased each other. Chloe felt the curious stares as they continued to walk down the street.

"I thought we would do a little exploring," Gary explained. He stuffed his hands deep into his pockets as they walked. Chloe remembered walking hand in hand with him. She quickly pushed the longing away.

"What about Brent and Jennifer? I was hired to chaperone the girl."

"They'll be fine. I told them to be on board The Bounty by two o'clock. That's only a few hours for them to explore—more than enough time to see everything, not enough time to get into trouble."

Chloe wasn't so sure, but she didn't argue. Instead, she forced her attention to her beautiful surroundings. Thick foliage lined one side of the street. Sand followed by ocean waves opened to the other side of the street. It was a tropical paradise.

"What's the sigh for?" Gary asked.

Chloe hadn't realized she'd sighed. How could she explain it? The salty air, tropical breeze, a beautiful, foreign port—it was wonderful. "I wish I could freeze this moment, put it in my pocket, and take it out when I feel unhappy."

Gary didn't comment. Instead, he cautiously took Chloe's hand. He held it loosely, allowing her to pull away if she wanted. Her heart picked up speed at his touch. She knew he wanted to make up for the hurt he caused her, but there was nothing he could do. For now she wanted to pretend none of the animosity existed between them. She wanted to be at peace with Gary. She didn't pull her hand away. She didn't look at him. Instead, they continued to walk along the quiet road.

They passed a small, dilapidated house the size of a shack.

There were no glass panes in the window. Two old broken-down cars were parked in the yard. There were also a few bikes, and a skinny dog barked at them as they walked near. "I'm glad I don't live there," Chloe commented. "Without windowpanes, it would be impossible to keep the dirt out."

"I would imagine dirt is the least of their concerns," Gary commented.

"Look at that," Chloe said, pointing to a stone building several yards up the road from them. The building looked old yet well cared for. Vines grew up the walls and over the roof. "I don't think it's a house."

Curious, they approached the building. People were coming out, and they appeared to be tourists. "I think it might be a church," Gary guessed as they walked up the stone path to the open double doors.

The walls of the church were made from rough stone, and the windows were stained glass. It was a small building that apparently welcomed tourists. People milled about the foyer and beyond in the sanctuary. Chloe and Gary stepped cautiously through the foyer and into the most unusual sanctuary. It was actually an open courtyard with flowering bushes, trees, and tropical flowers. An altar was placed in the middle of the courtyard with two bubbling fountains on either side. Little birds darted into the flowering bushes and back out. It was beautiful.

"Buenos días. Welcome to Shepherd's Fold Christian Church."

Both Chloe and Gary turned at the sound of the pleasant yet thickly accented voice. It was an older woman who spoke to them. She wore a long, dark dress, and her graying hair was pulled into a knot at the back of her head. She stared at Chloe and Gary with sparkling, dark eyes. "You are from the States, sí?"

Gary and Chloe both nodded. "Yes, Texas actually."

The woman motioned them to follow her. "Come, sign our guest form. We like to have a record of everyone who visits us. My husband, the pastor, wants to pray for all our guests."

Chloe and Gary followed her from the courtyard sanctuary back into the dark stone foyer. "Many visitors get married in our little chapel. Tourists like it. It's very romantic, sí?"

Chloe nodded. "Yes, very beautiful."

The woman pointed to several different papers on a small table. "This form is for church membership, but you won't want that. Here is a marriage certificate. And this form is for our guests to sign." Chloe peered at the forms the woman showed her, trying to feign interest. She didn't want to worry about signing in. She just wanted to enjoy the lovely sanctuary for a little longer before they had to go back to the boat.

"If you'll pardon me," the woman said, "I must speak with these people." She turned to greet the couple stepping into the foyer.

"I suppose we should sign one of these visitor forms to be polite," Chloe murmured.

Gary shrugged with disinterest. "Okay."

"Do you know which one she said was for visitors? I think she said this one." As Chloe reached for the form a ruckus broke out in the foyer. A little boy carrying a chicken walked into the church. He seemed to know what he was doing, but the chicken had other ideas. It wriggled itself loose from the boy's grasp and began flapping around the foyer. Someone screamed. Papers went flying. The little boy chased the chicken to no avail. Finally the bird found its freedom through the front doorway.

Chloe bent to pick up the scattered papers. Now they all looked the same to her. Each was written in Spanish, and she had no idea which went where on the table. She should have paid more attention!

"Can we go?" Gary asked impatiently.

"I'd like to go back to the sanctuary and take a picture of it. I've never seen a more beautiful church," Chloe pleaded. "We could add it to the Web site."

Gary conceded and led Chloe back into the sanctuary. She walked up to the altar and watched the water bubble in one of the fountains.

"Isn't it peaceful here? I can see why someone would want to come worship God in a place like this. All the world's troubles are left outside, and this comforting atmosphere draws you in and welcomes you."

"It certainly keeps you mindful of the beauty in God's creation," Gary agreed. He plucked a red flower from a bush and handed it to Chloe. He gave her an appreciative smile when she tucked it behind her ear. "It's like the Garden of Eden." Gary's gaze was warm and intent on Chloe's upturned face. She wondered if he was thinking about kissing her in this hidden sanctuary. She took a quick step away from him.

Others entered the sanctuary, breaking the tranquility. A large man strode over to Gary and Chloe. He was about the same age as the woman. His middle was round, and his hair was white. He reminded Chloe of Santa Claus; a tropical Santa Claus with a red flowered shirt. He shook Gary's hand and patted Chloe on the back.

"Buenos días!" he greeted, then rambled on in Spanish with both Chloe and Gary staring at him stupidly.

Not getting a response from either Gary or Chloe, the man pointed to the forgotten papers gripped in Chloe's fist. He handed her a pen.

"Oh! He wants us to sign the visitor form." Chloe shuffled through the papers, not recognizing the correct form. "If we sign the wrong paper, we'll be church members," she joked.

"Or married," Gary added. He pulled out one of the papers. "Just sign this one."

Chloe studied the paper, wishing she had taken Spanish as an elective rather than music appreciation. "Do you really think we should sign it?" she asked doubtfully. She didn't understand one word that was printed on the paper.

Gary shrugged. "It won't hurt anything. Besides, we need to get back to the boat."

"All right. I'll sign on the line." And with a flourish, Chloe signed her name then handed the pen to Gary. Without so much as glancing at the document Gary signed his name next to hers. Chloe noticed that his signature was long yet hastily penned. The signature suited him. He handed the paper to the man Chloe assumed was the pastor.

The Mexican clapped his hands together. "Bueno." He turned to Gary and asked, "Usted toma a este mujer como su esposa?"

Chloe could see Gary was perplexed and in danger of losing his patience. "Don't you know any Spanish?" she whispered.

Gary shook his head. "Unfortunately, no." He glanced at his watch. "I think we should be going. Let's just nod and smile, say thanks a few times, and go." Gary nodded to the pastor. "Sí, gracias. Buenos días."

Bewilderment flickered across the man's face at Gary's answer. He then turned to Chloe.

"Usted toma a este hombre como su marido?" He spoke the words slowly, but Chloe still didn't understand.

She shrugged then nodded. "You have a beautiful church. We've enjoyed visiting. Gracias."

A wide smile broke out across the pastor's face. "Ahora le declaro marido y esposa. El Dios le bendice!" He clapped Gary on the back, hugged Chloe then ushered them to the door.

"Vaya con Dios," he said as he handed Gary the signed paper.

"What just happened?" Gary asked, mystified.

"I'm not sure. I thought we were complimenting him on his lovely church," Chloe answered, equally confused.

"I have the feeling that we didn't sign a visitor's form."

As they passed into the foyer Gary sought out the Mexican woman. "Can you explain this to me?" he asked, shoving the signed paper into the woman's hands.

The woman handed the form back to Gary. "You have signed the marriage certificate. My husband, the pastor, has joined his signature with yours. You are married. Congratulations!"

Gary shook his head and tried to hand the paper back to the woman. "We aren't married. It's not possible. I didn't understand a word that man said!"

"Is it legal?" Chloe asked, feeling as stricken as Gary looked.

"This certificate is accepted in the eyes of the church. You are married," the woman answered gently.

"Can't we go back and tell him it was a mistake?" Gary asked. "We signed the wrong form. Nothing he said to us made sense."

"Young man, how can you say it was a mistake? You love her. Love shines in your eyes. God brought you here, and you were joined as one in His house. There is no mistake. Entiende? Do you understand?"

A long silence ensued as Gary stared at the marriage certificate. Finally he nodded. "Yes, I understand."

Gary and Chloe stepped out into the bright sunlight and slowly walked down the stone path to the road. Neither of them spoke though many questions hung in the air. Chloe watched as little children, half dressed in the heat, darted into the path in front of them. Their giggles and rapid Spanish helped to lift Chloe's somber mood. It was too difficult to fathom what had taken place in the little Mexican church, yet she knew God would take care of them. Somehow it would all be resolved.

It was strange. She walked into the unusual church as a tourist, and she walked out as. . .

Mrs. Gary Erickson.

An overwhelming surge of fear and dismay flowed through her. It wasn't possible. She couldn't be married to Gary! He didn't love her. If he didn't care enough six years ago, how could he possibly care now? She could only imagine what Gary was thinking. He was probably furious. It was her fault they were in such an impossible situation. If she hadn't gone back into the sanctuary for a picture then they wouldn't have met the pastor. One thing would not have led to another.

"We should hurry back to the boat," Gary said with a glance at his watch. "I hope no one has missed us. We've been gone longer than I anticipated." His tone was terse, and Chloe knew he wasn't pleased. She couldn't blame him. She didn't feel that great, either.

"Gary, about what happened back there—"

"Do you really want to talk about it right now? I think we should just forget about it since there isn't anything we can do at the moment."

Chloe swallowed her disappointment. Part of her hoped he would be a little more understanding or even interested in the fact that they were married. Every girl dreamed of being married in an unusual way—swept off her feet by someone she loved.

No! I do not still love him! I just got caught up in the romance of the moment. Gary Erickson is the man who purposely broke my heart. And he would do it again, given the chance.

Gary picked up his pace, and Chloe nearly had to jog to keep up with him. Finally she gave up. It wasn't worth it to try to appease him. He would have to deal with the situation, and so would she. She just preferred to turn to the Lord.

As Gary strode ahead without noticing Chloe lagging behind, Chloe decided it was time to cast her cares upon the Lord's wide shoulders. It didn't matter to her that children gave her curious stares as she talked to herself. She needed help!

"Lord, You know the desires of my heart. If I were to marry, my husband would have to be strong yet kind. Patient yet easily humored. He would have to be a man of faith and wisdom. And he can't be a liar." Chloe sighed. "I don't feel that it's wrong we married. We didn't know what we were doing. But I don't know how we can continue. He doesn't love me anymore. And I—well, I feel like I have a heart of stone. Help us to resolve this—and without pain. Amen."

Chloe breathed a sigh of relief when she saw The Bounty moored at the pier. Nothing ever looked so good as the boat she had spent several weeks on. There had been several times she wished she could step off the boat and never return. But at the moment she couldn't wait to feel the rocking deck beneath her feet. She wanted to lock herself in her stateroom and consider what to do about Gary. Having her mother there would have made the situation much easier. Mom always knew what to do.

As they approached the boat, Gary suddenly stopped and waited for Chloe to catch up with him. "For now, say nothing about this to anyone." He folded up the marriage certificate and slipped it into his wallet. "We'll figure it all out later." He gave her a grim nod then preceded her as they walked up the gangplank.

On the boat they found Brent and Jennifer in the salon.

Jennifer flipped through a magazine while Brent shuffled a deck of cards. Jennifer didn't look up as they came in, but Brent greeted them profusely.

"Hey! Glad you're back. You two sure disappeared fast. Get any good bargains? There's tons of stuff to buy out there. The beer is dirt cheap, too. Did you get any, Professor Gary?" Brent asked.

"Uh, no. Where did you two go? We didn't see you." Chloe figured he was trying to divert Brent's curiosity. The last thing either of them wanted to discuss was the counterfeit wedding.

An uncomfortable silence followed, and Jennifer visibly stiffened. Something wasn't right. Jennifer kept her eyes averted. She was hiding something or was terribly upset. Brent wasn't behaving normally either. He didn't usually show Gary so much enthusiasm.

"We went here and there," Brent evaded. "We've been back for an hour. Is there something you need me to do?"

Gary shook his head. "Uh, no. Thanks, Brent. Has anyone tracked Daisy since we've been in port? We don't want to lose her."

Silence greeted him.

Gary sighed in frustration. "Okay. I'll take care of it." He went over to the computer and logged on. While he was pulling up the program on the computer, a meaningful glance passed between Brent and Jennifer. Chloe wondered what was going on between them. She hoped it didn't mean Jennifer would get hurt. Chloe knew the girl's heart was involved.

"Did you and the professor have a good time?" Brent asked Chloe. "You two spend a lot of time together these days."

Chloe shifted uncomfortably under Brent's piercing gaze. "I don't know what you're talking about." She purposely ignored Brent and turned her attention to Jennifer. "Did you spend a lot of time out in the sun, Jennifer? You look a little burned."

"Of course I burned! I always burn!" Jennifer snapped as she turned her attention back to her magazine.

Chloe stared at Jennifer in surprise. She'd never heard her speak a harsh word. Something wasn't right. Chloe dug in her tote for some aloe lotion. Jennifer was probably irritable because of the burn.

"Hey, Chloe! Come rub some of that lotion on my shoulders. I got burned, too," Brent taunted. He gave Chloe a flirtatious wink. "Take pity on me. I might blister without that cooling lotion."

I doubt that. She handed him the bottle of lotion. Brent tossed it back to her.

"Come on, Chloe. Be a sport, and put it on for me. I'd hate to miss a spot." He pulled off his shirt, revealing a tanned back and chest. To his credit, his shoulders were lightly pink.

Not wanting to make a fuss, Chloe calmly did as she was bid. She squirted some of the creamy lotion into her hand then cautiously dabbed the lotion on Brent's shoulders. Once she finished her hasty job she looked up to find Gary scowling at her from his seat behind the computer.

"Can I talk to you outside, Chloe?" Gary ground out. He shoved back his chair and strode to the door.

Chloe hurried after him, wondering how she would handle this latest blunder.

"I wasn't flirting with him," she blurted as she closed the sliding glass door. "He asked me to put lotion on him, and what was I supposed to do? He put me in a difficult position. I didn't know what to do."

Gary held up his hand. "He manipulated you. I'm not mad at you, all right? The reason I called you out here is to ask if you noticed anything odd about the way Brent and Jennifer are acting."

Chloe breathed a sigh of relief. "Yes! Jennifer is clearly upset about something. She's never said a harsh word before today. Brent seems normal, though," she added with a grimace.

"I think we need to watch them. Something is going on, but I have no idea what it is. As Jennifer's chaperone, you need to stick close to her. Put some distance between her and Brent. I'll tell your uncle to keep his eyes open, too." Gary shoved his hands deep into his pockets in a gesture of frustration. His scowl deepened.

Chloe wished she could smooth away the creases caused by Gary's frown. He was such a handsome man—but she didn't want to think about that! "Why don't I try to talk with Jennifer?" Chloe suggested, forcing her thoughts back to the matter at hand. "She's clearly upset. Maybe I can get her to confide in me."

"If you think it'll help, give it a try." He paused, crossing his arms over his chest. "Now, why don't we talk about what happened in that little church this afternoon?"

Chloe blanched, taking a step back. She didn't want to talk about what happened. It was easier to pretend nothing had happened. "I don't think that's such a good idea. You wanted to forget about it until it can be resolved, and that's what I plan to do."

Gary shook his head. His blue eyes became aquamarine as his gaze pierced hers. It was impossible for her to look away. "I think you're scared," he challenged, taking a step toward her.

Please, Lord! Chloe silently prayed. Help me! She took another step back as Gary advanced toward her. She felt a chair behind her and dropped onto the seat. Gary towered over her. Silence stretched between them as he stared intently at her. Chloe wished she could disappear, run—anything. But she couldn't move. Gary's intense blue eyes held her gaze. She was powerless to leave or protest as her breathing came in short, uneven gasps. Was she scared? Yes!

Gary leaned closer until only inches separated them. "Why don't you want to admit that you are my wife?"

seven

Chloe couldn't believe Gary had said the word. It was impossible—like a bad dream, but Chloe knew by the way her heart was pounding that she wasn't dreaming. Gary had just called her his wife.

She pulled her gaze from his as warmth drew up her neck and into her cheeks. She knew she was as red as Jennifer's sunburn, and she felt just as uncomfortable. Only Chloe's pain didn't come from her skin, it came from her heart. "You can't be serious, Gary. You're the one who didn't want to talk about it, and I agree. Whatever happened in that little church didn't really happen! We're not married!"

She could feel the panic rising within her chest. She was not Mrs. Gary Erickson. He was the last man she wanted to marry. He didn't love her. He didn't want her. All of the things Trevor had said came back to her like a flood tide. Her appearance wasn't suitable. She didn't deal well with people in public. No man would ever desire her for his wife. Her father thought she was an expensive burden. She was impractical. Tiresome. Chloe sank lower in her seat. Her shoulders sagged in defeat, and her gaze dulled. No, she couldn't be Gary's wife. Even if she had wanted to at one time, it was impossible now.

Gary pulled the paper with both their signatures out of his wallet. "This is a marriage certificate, and it says we are married."

"How do you know what it says? You can't read Spanish any better than I can," Chloe mumbled, crossing her arms over her chest. "I don't think you should believe it." She added silently to herself, And now you can feel free of any obligation, Gary. I know you would never choose to be married to me. "Let's forget the silly thing ever happened."

Gary carefully folded the paper and stuffed it into his shirt pocket. "Just because I can't read it doesn't mean it's false. I just wanted to talk to you about it to see if you had any ideas on how we should deal with this unusual situation," he answered calmly.

When Chloe declined to answer, Gary continued a bit more testily. "Look, I'm sorry you find yourself stuck with me in this mess. I didn't plan it; believe me! You think I'm happy being married to a. . .a man-hater?"

Chloe's chin raised a notch, but she still didn't answer. Fine. She knew where she stood. It was easier to let him believe she hated men. Gary didn't care for her and didn't want to be married to her. So as far as she was concerned, they weren't married. They weren't anything. She wondered how she was going to avoid him for the remainder of the trip. Maybe if she worked at night, communicated through notes, somehow she would finish out her responsibility with as little contact as possible. It would be easier than trying to deal with this difficult man.

"Give me the paper, please," Chloe demanded, holding out her hand. There was one way to take care of this problem. If the paper didn't exist, neither did their sham of a marriage. No one needed to know they were married in a little Mexican church. If they forgot the ordeal, then it wouldn't really exist. Neither of them felt married, anyway.

"Why do you want it? So you can tear up the certificate? I'm not going to let you do that. We can't pretend this didn't happen." It was as though he had heard her inner thoughts.

Chloe withdrew her hand, scowling at Gary. Why did he

have to be so difficult? He asked her to keep the ceremony a secret from the others. It was clear he didn't want the marriage. Why was he so adamant to resolve it now?

Gary shoved his hand through his already mussed hair. "It's obvious you don't want to deal with this, and I can't talk to you when you act this way. So we'll forget it for now. You do your job. I'll do mine. If you want, when we get home I'll contact a lawyer and see what we need to do about this."

"Fine," Chloe mumbled through gritted teeth. "But promise me you won't tell my uncle or anyone else. We can't let this get out. Just like you said earlier, we'll keep it to ourselves."

Chloe expected Gary to glare at her, but his gaze softened. "I promise you, honey, you have nothing to fear. This is between just you and me."

☙

"It's time to go!" Uncle Howard called from his seat behind the helm. Gary wasn't in sight. Chloe imagined he was below in his stateroom, avoiding her. She watched Brent untie the boat and hop back on board. He didn't look happy either. Normally he had an interested if not humored smirk on his face. The smirk was replaced with a frown that knitted his brow. At Brent's signal the boat engines started with a roar, and Uncle Howard pulled away from the pier. Brent surprised Chloe by coming toward her and flopping down on the bench next to her.

"What's going on, Brent?"

Brent shook his head, his lips pressed in a firm, angry line. "I wasn't ready to leave. I don't think it's a good idea."

"Why not? The engines seem to be in good working order. Why would you want to stay here? What did you and Jennifer do today?"

Brent eased closer to Chloe; his shoulder rubbed hers. "Are you jealous of Jennifer? I could have spent the day with you instead." He grinned down at her, and Chloe knew it was the hundred-watt smile that was supposed to melt her heart. She stiffened and inched away on the seat.

She could easily understand how he affected Jennifer. Brent was a handsome guy and very charismatic. And too young for Chloe no matter what Brent might think. Four years might not be a wide span of their ages, but Chloe felt much older than Brent. She needed a man with spiritual depth, mature in his thinking and understanding. She wanted someone like— Chloe refused to allow her mind to produce his name.

"You should find someone your own age—a nice girl." She didn't like the way he was looking at her, like a starving man in search of a meal.

"You're a nice girl, Chloe." He trailed his finger along her shoulder, allowing his touch to rest on the thin gold chain around her neck.

"Brent, I'm not interested—"

"I'm interested, very interested, in you."

Chloe scooted farther away from Brent and pushed his hand away. "You can't be interested in me! Remember what Gary said?"

"Do you think it matters to me what Gary says? He doesn't dictate what I do with my personal time and my private thoughts. He's my boss for the next several weeks, but he doesn't control me." Brent resumed touching the gold chain at Chloe's neck as though he were trying to wear down her resistance.

Chloe wished she shared his confidence when it came to dealing with Gary. In some ways she longed for Gary. He had swept her off her feet—shown her how wonderful love could be. She wondered if they could possibly share that kind of love again. It seemed so long ago, and she was a different person now. If given the chance could she even feel so intensely again? She wasn't sure she was capable of such emotion. That side of her was buried when she mourned the loss of Gary's love. Could it be resurrected? The Bible said nothing is impossible for God. Did she dare believe that perhaps God had given them another chance?

"Will you show me your necklace?" Brent asked suddenly. He fingered the chain, drawing it away from her neck.

Chloe grasped the heart-shaped locket and showed it to Brent. "My mother gave it to me. Right now it's empty. I'm hoping to fill it with a picture of my hus—husband someday." She stumbled over the word as Gary's image came to mind. According to the Mexican church, she already had a husband. Somehow she didn't think his picture could fit into her tiny locket.

"I think I'd better go work on lunch. It's my turn in the kitchen." She jumped to her feet and hurried away.

❧

Chloe made lunch into a more elaborate affair than she first intended. She wouldn't dare admit that she'd gone to extra lengths to please Gary. He probably wouldn't notice, anyway.

She took her time and made pasta with mahimahi and a light, creamy sauce. After adding different spices, she was finally pleased with her culinary creation.

She called Brent to tell him lunch was ready then went in search of Jennifer. Chloe found her down in her stateroom. Jennifer was in her bed huddled beneath the blankets.

"Jennifer, are you sick?"

"No!" came her sniffling response.

Puzzled, Chloe stepped closer. "If you're not sick then what's wrong?"

"Have you ever felt like you're going to die of a broken heart?" Jennifer sniffed again.

"I certainly have. And sometimes, even though I don't

think I have any heart left to break, I feel like it keeps pulling apart."

Jennifer sat upright, throwing off the covers. "That's exactly how I feel! Every time he talks to you, I feel like my battered heart breaks a little more," Jennifer whispered through her tears. "It's because I'm fat."

Chloe sat on the edge of the bed and patted Jennifer's hand. She hoped the Lord would give her the right words to encourage the girl. Chloe knew what it was like to suffer, and she didn't want Jennifer to feel any more pain. "I want you to listen to me. Remember when we talked about finding a man who sees the real treasure in us? Brent isn't that man. He sees only what he wants to see. He doesn't see true beauty. You need a man who will delight in you, regardless of your size or coloring. Please, for the rest of the trip, try not to think about superficial things. Set your heart to enjoying the task at hand. Then your heart won't ache so much, and Brent won't be able to hurt you like this."

"It isn't that easy," Jennifer whined.

"I know it isn't. But for God, everything is easy. Can I pray with you? I know God will ease your pain if you want Him to."

Jennifer nodded and wiped her teary eyes. "Okay, Chloe. I want Him to."

Chloe took Jennifer's hand and said, "Lord, You are the God of comfort, and You desire Jennifer to walk in Your peace. I pray You will comfort her and replace this anguish she feels. You know the right man for her. He is someone who will honor her and cherish her. He will see her value and will encourage her and bless her. Help her to keep her eyes on You. I pray You will help Jennifer to be friends with Brent. She can be a friend to him and bless him without needing anything in return. I thank You for her, and I thank You for all the things You've done for her. In Jesus' name, amen."

Chloe felt herself answering amen to the prayer on her own behalf. She wanted the same things Jennifer was looking for.

"It's time for lunch," Chloe said, forcing her thoughts to more practical issues.

"Thanks, Chloe."

She paused in the doorway. "One more thing—I'd like to talk to you about your trip into town today." Chloe noticed Jennifer stiffen but decided to press the issue anyway. "I know Brent is into something, and I'd hate to see you get in trouble as well. If you'll discuss it with me, maybe together we can come up with a plan that will help everyone." She left on that note, hoping Jennifer would agree to confide in her.

ð

Chloe filled three plates with the steaming pasta for Uncle Howard, herself, and one for Gary. Uncle Howard was in the pilothouse, standing at the helm. He pointed to a flat, empty spot on the console for Chloe to set the plate.

"Everything okay, Chloe-girl? You haven't been talking as much," her uncle observed.

Chloe shrugged evasively. "Everything's fine. Maybe I can come back later for a chat. I have to deliver more food to this hungry crew."

"No doubt to the professor, I suspect. Go settle yourself with him and enjoy your lunch. We'll talk some other time."

Chloe found Gary up on the flybridge. He was staring at the horizon, deep in thought. In the moments he was unaware of her presence, Chloe was able to appraise him. He wore jean shorts, a navy T-shirt with the university's logo on it, and dark sunglasses. Chloe was glad she didn't have to see his blue eyes. They did funny things to her insides. His blond hair peeked out from under a red ball cap. He needed a shave, but the rugged look was appealing to Chloe. She sighed. *I don't want to find anything appealing about Gary. I'm no* different than Jennifer. I'm pining over a man I should never consider.

Gary turned, his gaze softening. "Did you need something?"

Chloe held up the two plates of pasta. "I brought your lunch."

"Come sit by me." He patted the seat next to him. Chloe settled on the bench, careful to leave enough space between them. Wordlessly they began eating. Chloe felt herself relax and actually enjoy being near Gary.

"About the marriage certificate. . ."

Gary shook his head. "Let's not worry about that just yet." He pointed with his fork at his plate of food. "This is wonderful." He took another bite of the fish. "Where did you learn to cook like this? Remember the brownies you made for me? They were as hard and black as charcoal."

Chloe returned his impish smile. "And you ate three of them without a word of complaint." She couldn't help looking at him fondly. "Mom and I have spent many hours in the kitchen together since then. I don't have too many cooking disasters now. It's become something of a hobby."

"This is like tasting heaven," Gary added as he finished off his pasta. "I'd like to sample more of your cooking if it's all this good. Is it possible?" His gaze had gone from teasing to wistful.

Chloe swallowed, realizing they were turning a new corner in their conversation—perhaps in their relationship. Could she do it? It would be easy to protect her heart and turn him down. He deserved to be rejected, she reasoned. But God's way was the best way.

"I think anything is possible," Chloe answered with a tentative smile. It was difficult to meet his gaze, but she forced herself to anyway. She was rewarded with the hopeful glimmer that lit his eyes.

"Anything, Chloe? Is anything really possible?"

"Anything is possible with God," she answered with conviction.

Gary smiled.

⁂

That evening they docked in the port town of La Pesca. Uncle Howard had a favorite restaurant near the marina in the center of all the tourist shops. Everyone seemed to be in high spirits. Chloe knew why she was cheerful, and it had everything to do with a certain professor. She didn't know what the future held, but for now she was content.

"I've heard about these types of restaurants, Chloe," Jennifer said in a conspiratorial whisper. "You take one bite of food, and your mouth is on fire for the rest of the night—not to mention your belly."

Uncle Howard gave her a wink, and Chloe knew what Jennifer said was true. "Why don't we go shopping, Jennifer? These men can enjoy the cuisine without us."

Despite protests from the men, Chloe and Jennifer went in a different direction with promises to meet up later.

As they walked past the first two stores, shop owners called to them from the doorways. They held up T-shirts and beaded necklaces, trying to tempt Chloe and Jennifer into their stores.

One particular shop drew Chloe's interest. They had several brightly colored garments hanging in the front of the store. "Let's go there."

Chloe browsed through some skirts and found a red one with a white sea turtle pattern stamped on the material. It would go perfectly over her swimsuit. Next she picked out an ankle bracelet made of silver turtles.

"Lady likes turtles?"

Chloe turned, finding a slender man not much taller than

her. His dark hair was slicked back, and his deep-set eyes studied her like a hawk. Chloe shifted uncomfortably under his gaze. "Um, yes. I do like turtles."

"Come with me," he said in thickly accented English. "I show more turtles." He motioned for Chloe to follow him to the back of the store.

"Oh. Well, all right," Chloe answered uneasily. She was thankful Jennifer filed in behind her as she ducked behind the ratty orange curtain that separated the storefront from the rear.

The back room was cramped and dimly lit by a bare hanging bulb. It was hot and muggy. Perspiration broke out on Chloe's upper lip, and she wasn't sure if it was because of the heat or her nerves. It wasn't a good situation to be in. She knew it. When she spotted the merchandise on the shelves, Chloe knew why she didn't feel right about being there.

"Chloe, look!" Jennifer gasped. She picked up a necklace made from the shells of baby turtles. The shells were connected end to end, forming a circle. Chloe saw earrings and pendants. Larger shells were used for bowls. Leather boots were made out of the soft flippers of sea turtles.

"Have you ever seen anything like this?" Chloe asked in horror.

"Actually, yes. Brent and I went to a place—"

Chloe looked at her sharply and wanted to question her about what she had seen with Brent, when the shop owner interrupted.

"You buy something, sí?" The man's voice held a threatening edge. He shoved a pair of turtle earrings into Chloe's hands. "You buy."

Chloe pushed the earrings away from her and backed up, bumping against the shelf behind her. "No! I mean, I don't think so." A stroke of fear shot through her stomach and up into her throat. She felt she might choke in fright. The man glared at her, and Chloe suddenly realized she and Jennifer might be in danger. No one knew where they were.

The man shoved the earrings in Jennifer's face. "You buy! Twenty-five American dollars."

Jennifer shook her head. "No, gracias!" She backed toward the curtain, pulling Chloe with her. Chloe noticed Jennifer's fingers were shaking as much as her own.

The man grabbed Jennifer's arm in a steel grip. "You buy!"

"No!" someone bellowed from behind them.

Both Chloe and Jennifer turned and gaped at the sound of the thunderous voice. The orange curtain was jerked back, and Howard Statton filled the doorway.

&

"How did you know where to find us, Uncle Howard?" Chloe asked as they walked down the dusty street toward the restaurant. Darkness was falling, and the shadows were growing. Chloe quickened her steps.

"I noticed you girls heading that way and thought I'd keep an eye on you. I've had problems with that particular shop before. At least the policia didn't have to get involved this time."

Chloe shivered. If her uncle hadn't shown up when he did. . .

Howard rested his heavy hand on Chloe's shoulder. "God is the one to protect you. You have nothing to fear when your trust is in Him."

Chloe breathed a heartfelt sigh. "I know. It was an awful place, though. All those poor turtles—doesn't that man realize all sea turtles are endangered and under protection?"

Howard chuckled and hugged Chloe to his side. "Those men don't care about such things! I'm just glad he showed you the turtles and not all the drugs he pushes. Next time someone invites you into a back room, you leave the shop. Understand me, girls?"

Both Chloe and Jennifer nodded, thankful Howard had been there to rescue them.

ð

Feeling subdued and no longer interested in festivities, Chloe and Jennifer reluctantly joined the men at the restaurant. Howard found two empty chairs and pulled them up to the round table for the girls. Chloe found herself pressed next to Gary. He had a half-eaten burrito, smothered in thick green chili sauce, sitting in front of him.

"I ate the whole thing!" Brent bragged as Chloe and Jennifer sat on the rickety wooden chairs. "And I only had to drink three bottles of water."

Jennifer giggled, apparently already forgetting their terrible experience. Chloe couldn't bring herself to join in the merriment. The sight of all those turtles. . . It was so disheartening.

"Something happened?" Gary asked just loud enough for Chloe to hear him.

Chloe turned, reading the concern in his eyes. "Yes, but I don't think I want to talk about it now."

Gary rose, pulling Chloe from her seat. He turned to Howard. "Will you make sure these two make it back to the boat tonight?" he said, motioning to Jennifer and Brent. "I'm going to take Chloe back now."

Howard nodded, giving Chloe a friendly wink. She returned a slight smile. "Thanks again, Uncle Howard. You have no idea."

"Sure I do, Chloe-girl. Now try to get that business you saw out of your mind. It isn't worth fretting about since you can't change it. And on your way back, don't forget to notice the stars. They're beautiful in this part of the world."

Gary took ahold of Chloe's hand and led her out of the restaurant. He didn't release his grasp once they were outside. Instead of striking out at a quick pace as Chloe was accustomed, Gary set a leisurely rate. After a few yards he released

Chloe's hand, and she immediately regretted the lost contact. Then he wrapped his arm around her shoulders.

"Do you want to tell me what happened?" he asked.

Chloe sighed. Images of turtle shell necklaces and bowls flashed through her mind. Everything Gary worked for people to understand was destroyed in that hot, sticky back room. "No, I don't want to tell you." She felt Gary withdraw from her, so she added quickly, "I don't want to talk about it, but I feel like you should know what we saw." She told him about the various turtle artifacts, then said, "I think what bothers me most is the total disregard for one of God's creatures. They are beautiful, gentle animals being hunted for their shells. It's terrible."

Gary hugged her against his side. "Did Howard tell you how he knows about that place?"

Chloe shook her head. "No. He just said he's had a run-in with those people before and mentioned something about them being involved in drug trafficking. What are you thinking?"

"I think someone on board is involved with poachers."

"You aren't accusing my uncle, are you? He'd never sell turtles to a poacher!" The words passed her lips but were quickly followed by doubts. How well did she really know her uncle? She had spent very little time with him over the years. Maybe some of her father's accusations were not so farfetched.

"Hey, slow down," Gary said, catching ahold of her hand again. "Take a moment and look at the stars. They're so bright."

Chloe stilled, realizing her uncle had said the same thing minutes earlier. She pushed all thoughts of him out of her mind. Tilting her head back, Chloe was amazed at all the stars she could see. "I wish things were simpler. I wish I could just reach up and take the stars in my hands."

"They remind me of the light dancing in your eyes," Gary whispered.

Chloe turned to stare deeply into Gary's eyes. "Why did you say that?"

"I guess because you help me forget the ugly things. I feel like a poet. All things are possible with God, right?"

Chloe sighed. "The Bible says so, and I have to stand on that. It's just that not everything turns out the way I hope. My life has not been a fairy tale."

"I'd like to make that different, Chloe. I don't even know how to start. It seems that I'm always saying and doing the wrong thing when it comes to dealing with you. I went crazy with jealousy over Brent. I hated having him fawn over you."

"I don't know where to go from here. I'm scared to trust you. Maybe we should just be friends."

Gary studied her in the dim light. In a gentle movement he tucked a stray wisp of hair behind her ear. "I'll be satisfied with whatever I can get. And I'll thank God daily for the friendship you give me."

His answer perplexed her. He wasn't supposed to be kind. He was the heartbreaker. "What has changed with you, Gary? Why do you suddenly care?"

"No matter what you think, I've never stopped caring."

Chloe didn't have an answer. As she silently pondered his words they continued walking to the marina. Dim lights flickered along the pier where The Bounty was docked. Gary stopped suddenly, causing Chloe to bump into him.

"What is it?"

Gary pointed at the boat. "Someone is on the boat."

Chloe peered at the figure lounging on the rear deck. He was familiar. Even in the darkness she recognized him. Inwardly, she groaned, not realizing the sound had escaped her lips.

"You know who it is?" Gary asked, tensely studying her face.

Chloe nodded reluctantly. "Yes. It's Trevor Renolds." She wondered if things could get any more complicated.

eight

It's about time you arrived. Where have you been?" Trevor asked as Chloe approached the boat. He stood and stuffed his hands into the pockets of his expensive slacks. Even though it was around one hundred degrees, Trevor looked cool and tidy. Every hair was in place. His white dress shirt was still crisp with creases. Trevor glared at her, and his look was almost as sharp as if he had slapped her.

Chloe winced but didn't say anything. She could read through Trevor's tight words. He was angry. A tirade was coming, and there was nothing she could do to prevent it. The best she could do was weather the storm then see what reparations she could make later.

Gary's hand tightened on hers as he helped her onto the boat. She was glad he didn't say anything. She had enough to deal with without having to appease him, too.

"It's just like you to be so irresponsible, Chloe. I hope this is the last foolish thing you do. Going off on some boat to find sea turtles! You have no idea the problems you left behind. You shirk all your responsibilities like a child!"

"How did you get here? How did you find me?" Chloe asked, hoping to defuse some of Trevor's outburst. She tried to ignore the terrible things Trevor was saying to her. It was humiliating having Gary standing next to her as Trevor harped on her every shortcoming.

"You look terrible, Chloe."

Chloe patted her hair self-consciously. Dark wisps of hair had escaped her ponytail and now floated around her face.

Perspiration dotted her forehead and upper lip. Her shorts and old T-shirt were rumpled and clung to her body in the sticky heat. She could imagine what Trevor thought of her appearance. At least he didn't elaborate on his disapproval. She wished she could have changed into something more presentable before having to face him. "You didn't say how you found me."

"You're not very hard to locate. That Web site tells every move you're going to make. I figured if I didn't come across you here, I would hire a boat to track you down. I felt it necessary to find you. You didn't answer my E-mail. Your father—"

Chloe's head snapped up, and her gaze locked with his. "What about my father?"

Trevor raised his eyebrows as he looked down his nose at her. "He's had some heart problems. The doctors say he'll be just fine, but they are monitoring his condition. With all the stress of his work and then with you running off, it has taken a toll on his heart."

Fear, intermingled with guilt, wrapped itself around Chloe's heart. Had her father taken on extra pressure because of her? The thought was too much to bear! She wasn't there to cover the utilities and other small bills. Her father always called her a burden, but now he must realize all she had contributed. Hopefully they weren't having financial troubles. Her father would never forgive her!

"I've made arrangements to fly you home tomorrow afternoon," Trevor continued. "I've got two rooms at a hotel an hour from here. It's not the best place. This dive didn't have much to offer," he complained.

Chloe nodded. Trevor was right. She should return home to take care of her father. She never should have left. Chloe wondered why her mother never said anything about her father's health in all of her correspondence. Mom probably didn't want to worry her.

"Now go pack up your things so we can get back to the hotel. I've got a driver waiting to take us. You probably don't have any proper clothing with you, so we'll have to come up with something in town tomorrow before we catch the flight back. Your father will be waiting for us at the airport." Trevor stopped, gazing at Chloe. "Why aren't you moving? Go pack!"

Chloe jumped at Trevor's barked order, but Gary stopped her from leaving with gentle pressure on her arm. He kept ahold of it as he turned his attention to Trevor.

"If her father is doing so poorly, why is he the one picking you up at the airport?" he asked in a calm yet direct way. His gaze pinned Trevor.

Gary's observation clearly caught Trevor off guard, but he was quick to recover. "I never said he was hospitalized. I just said he's had some troubles. As soon as Chloe returns, everything will be back to normal."

"And how will Chloe's return bring everything back to normal? Is he unable to work?"

Trevor shook his head reluctantly. His jaw tightened, and Chloe could tell he was furious. "No. He's still working the two jobs. But he has to take medication to control his condition, and the doctor visits have become more frequent." Trevor turned his gaze to Chloe. "He blames you, and I agree. You knew he didn't approve of you taking this trip, but you went anyway. You didn't do the right thing. If you'd stayed home, his heart troubles never would have happened."

"Enough!" Gary growled. "I've heard enough of your slandering. Mr. Crenshaw's heart condition has nothing to do with Chloe. Chloe is a grown woman, capable of making her own choices. She does not need anyone's approval to do what she wants."

Trevor turned red with anger, and Chloe knew he was

bout to explode. She put up her hand to intervene. "No. No, Trevor is right. If Dad needs me, then I should go back. It's not right for me to be having fun while he's carrying the burden of the family."

A muscle worked in Gary's jaw. Chloe couldn't remember him looking this frustrated. Yet he kept his emotions under control. With tight, even words he said, "While I'm glad you've enjoyed yourself on this expedition, you must remember that you've been working, Chloe. And I need you to continue working. If your dad can pick you up at the airport and continue working two jobs, then it doesn't sound like he really needs a hand from you. But if you want to go back, then I understand. I just don't want you leaving because you feel pressured to do so." Gary gave Trevor a pointed look. "I won't let you go just because he's coercing you."

Trevor clenched his teeth. "It's ridiculous that we're still discussing this. Chloe, pack your things!"

Chloe jumped at the sharp sound of his voice and hurried to the sliding glass door.

While she packed her belongings down in her stateroom, she heard Uncle Howard arrive with Brent and Jennifer. Chloe breathed a heavy sigh. It would have been easier to leave before they arrived. Now there would be an even bigger scene. Trevor always got his way.

"Lord, I don't want to go," she whispered. Tears trickled down her face. "I've enjoyed this trip so much. I feel that if I go home, I go into prison. But I know what Trevor says is right. My father blames me for his health. If I don't go, then it's the same as telling him I don't care. I want to stay, but I don't see how it's possible. Please help me, Lord."

After changing into a simple white sundress and combing her hair so it hung loose around her shoulders the way Trevor liked it, Chloe was ready to go. She grabbed her suitcase and

hefted it out of her room and up the stairs. Trevor hadn't
moved from his place on deck. He was talking with Uncle
Howard, and Chloe could see by Trevor's stance that he felt
defensive. The sooner she got him away from the boat the
better off everyone would be.

Gary entered the salon before Chloe could step out on the
deck.

"You look pretty in that dress. But why did you change?"
Gary asked.

Chloe fingered the buttons that ran down the length of
the dress. "I don't know. I guess I didn't feel suitable." Trevor
didn't think she looked suitable.

"You felt fine earlier. Why do you let him run you like
that?" His words weren't harsh or accusing. Instead, he was so
gentle that Chloe felt he was pitying her.

She raised her chin. Silence stretched between them as
Chloe debated whether to tell him the truth. It was something
she had never told anyone—something she hadn't wanted to
verbalize. "I suppose I should tell you. I accept his treatment—
his manipulation—on the basis that I have never loved him. I
never will love him, and I feel I owe him my cooperation in the
least." She stared intently at Gary, knowing she had to finish
what she started. "When you left me, I was never able to love
anyone else. I seriously doubt I'll ever love again."

"Do you really want to go?" Gary asked, taking a few steps
closer to her until she could see the pulse beating in his neck.

"No," she whispered. No, she didn't want to go. This expedition had been the most exciting time in her life. She wanted
to see it through and finish her job. She wanted to see the
nesting turtles. More than anything she wanted to know if
there was still a spark flickering between her and Gary. "But
my father expects me home, and Trevor has gone to a lot of
trouble because of me. I'm obligated to go."

"And what about your obligation to me? You agreed to work on this trip. I've counted on you, and you've done an outstanding job. I need you to finish."

Chloe felt torn between two necessities. If she chose to stay with the expedition, she may very well cut herself off from her father forever. But if she left now, she would always regret not finishing and wonder what she might have seen. "I don't know what to do."

"You don't have to do anything. Leave it all to me. You might not like this, but I'm about to make things a little more complicated. I believe you'll thank me someday."

Chloe frowned, not understanding what Gary was saying. He took the suitcase from her and shoved it against the wall. He then took ahold of her hand and pulled her out to the deck. The warm air hit her like a blast from a furnace, but she didn't notice the heat as much as the displeasure emanating from Trevor.

"Where are your things? We should be going," he demanded. "That driver will probably charge me a ridiculous amount of pesos for waiting so long."

Gary pulled Chloe against his side and wrapped his arm around her shoulders. "She's not going. She needs to stay here and finish what was begun."

Trevor blustered with indignation. "Who are you to say what she's doing? Her father needs her to come home and take care of him."

"I seriously doubt he needs anything from Chloe. Can't you let her make her own decision and enjoy herself? She's very capable, you know!"

Trevor's face turned an alarming shade of red. "Don't tell me what she's capable of! I'm her fiancé! She needs to come with me!"

"I know you're not her fiancé," Gary said calmly. He

squeezed Chloe's shoulders. She took in a jagged breath, praying this would end soon. Uncle Howard, Jennifer, and Brent were watching the scene play out as though this were their favorite soap opera.

"And how do you know I'm not her fiancé?" Trevor demanded. He pointed haughtily at Gary.

Trevor's airs of superiority didn't seem to bother Gary. He smiled confidently, and Chloe thought her heart would drop into her shoes. Chloe recognized the glimmer in his eyes. Gary was up to something. It was all a game, and he wasn't about to let Trevor win. Gary quirked an eyebrow at Chloe then turned back to Trevor. "I know you're not her fiancé," he answered calmly.

"Of course I'm her fiancé! Who are you to say otherwise?" Trevor spat.

Gary chuckled, and Chloe froze. "Don't, Gary!" she whispered.

He gave her shoulders a reassuring squeeze. "I know you're not her fiancé, because Chloe happens to be my wife."

A pin could have dropped in the silence that followed Gary's statement. Chloe stared at him in horror. He promised! It was a secret between them. He was going to take care of it when they reached the States. But it wasn't a secret anymore. Brent and Jennifer gaped at them, Uncle Howard chuckled, and Trevor—oh no, Trevor couldn't know! He would fly home and tell her parents! Her mom would be surprised, maybe disappointed. Her father would be furious!

A roaring sound filled Chloe's ears as the deck began to sway. She heard her uncle yell, "Catch her!" just before everything went dark.

❧

Chloe sat up, suddenly conscious. "Trevor! Where is he?" She realized she was lying on the leather sofa in the salon. "I need to explain."

Gary stood over her, shaking his head. "He's gone. He left in quite a huff, too."

Chloe leaned back against the sofa. "You told him we were—why did you tell him?"

Gary sagged onto the sofa next to her with a sigh. "I know we agreed to keep it a secret. That fool was so pompous. He was rude and demanding, and I couldn't let him have his way. Announcing our marriage was like having the trump card. He had to fold."

Chloe shook her head. "You're not making any sense. This isn't a game; it's my life. And right now Trevor is on his way back home to tell my parents that I've had a fling on this so-called foolish excursion. They'll never understand. I didn't want to break it to them like this. I didn't think I would have to tell them at all!"

Gary spread his hands in a helpless gesture. "I'm sorry, Chloe. It was spontaneous and completely out of character for me. The one thing that spurred my actions was that I couldn't let you go away—not like that—not with him."

"I would have been okay. I'm never going to marry Trevor."

"Because you don't love him?" Gary asked. His gaze was intent on her face.

"I never loved Trevor. He convinced me that we were right together. You must understand; Trevor is a very persuasive man. He didn't like me to make any decisions on my own. He is like my father in that he is difficult to please. It's tainted my view of men, I'm afraid."

"Understandable. And I haven't helped," Gary admitted with a frown.

Chloe sighed. "It isn't you. I think I bring out the worst in men. That's why it's probably best I stay single."

"But you aren't single anymore," Gary gently reminded.

Chloe started, realizing he was right. "I don't think—I

mean, you and me. . .we can't. . ." She gave up trying to convey her jumbled thoughts and stared at her hands, now clenched in her lap.

Gary scooted closer and took ahold of one of her hands. His hand was warm and strong, and he gently massaged his thumb over her fingers. "I certainly didn't expect it to happen," he commiserated as Chloe stared at him in surprise. "I'm sure you didn't plan your wedding day to be anything like that." Amusement crinkled the corners of his eyes as he glanced at Chloe.

Chloe was aware, once again, how attractive Gary was when he smiled. "I always wanted to get married someplace tropical. So that part happened. However I expected to be able to understand the minister. Instead I agreed to a lifelong commitment when all along I thought we were complimenting him on his church! It was a beautiful church," she added with a sigh.

Gary chuckled. It was a rich, pleasant sound from deep down. "That minister probably thought we were an odd couple. I didn't even kiss the bride."

Warmth filled Chloe's cheeks. "Not that time."

The look Gary gave her told her he remembered their brief kiss, too. "It's something I'd like to try again, if you'd let me."

It was a request Chloe didn't want to refuse. Her mind screamed the impossibilities as she stared deeply into his blue eyes. He would leave her again. He confused her, and she felt like she was on an emotional roller coaster. How could she trust him after so much had happened? Instead of heeding the protests, Chloe leaned closer to Gary. He drew her toward him and repeated the gentle kiss. It was even better than she remembered.

Chloe frowned as Gary released her. As much as she liked his kisses, they didn't solve the problem of Trevor rushing home to tell on her. Her parents would be distraught if she didn't do something.

"What should I do? My father is already stressed out. When he hears this, he'll go through the roof. I have no idea what condition he really is in. My mother. . ." Chloe dropped her gaze. "She'll never understand."

"I'm truly sorry about all this, Chloe. I wasn't thinking about your parents. I was only thinking about how wrong it was for Trevor Renolds to show up here, making ridiculous demands. He has a lot of nerve. I couldn't let you go with him. I need you here." He gave her a conciliatory smile. "We can still work through this even though it seems like a mess. Call your mom before Trevor has a chance to tell them anything. If your mom hasn't changed drastically, she'll be quick to understand."

His words had a calming effect on Chloe's frazzled nerves. "You're right. I need to talk to Mom—now!"

It seemed to take forever, but finally the call went through, and the phone was ringing. It was picked up on the third ring.

"Hello?" The sound of her mother's voice made Chloe's heart beat faster.

"Mom! It's me. I've got something to tell you." Chloe's fingers tapped out a nervous beat on the table. How could she tell her mom that she was now married? And to the man who broke her heart six years ago? Her mom wouldn't understand.

"Chloe, honey! It's so good to hear from you! I've been following your trip through the Internet site you showed me. And your letters have been so eventful! Are you having a good time?"

Chloe warmed to the comforting sound of her mom's voice, and she knew everything was going to be okay. "Yes, it has been fabulous. But, Mom, how is Dad feeling? Trevor was here." Her voice grew thick with agitation. "He said Dad was having heart problems and I needed to come home immediately."

Her mom gave a sigh of exasperation. "Your father has high blood pressure, along with a million other people in this world. He'll be fine."

"Does he need me to come home?"

"No! He's fine—a little grouchy, but that's nothing new," she said with a laugh. "You said Trevor flew down there?"

"Yes! He said Dad needed me home immediately," Chloe explained. She was beginning to put the facts together and realized Trevor had concocted another story to manipulate her.

"You aren't coming, are you? I think Trevor and your father were scheming again. Your dad still wants you to marry Trevor."

Chloe swallowed, remembering the reason for calling her mom. "Uh, Mom, it would be impossible to marry him."

"Oh, I agree! You can't marry him against your better judgment. He isn't the man God has for you."

"Mom, I need to tell you something. It's serious." Chloe took a deep breath, praying for courage. "I accidentally got married."

There was a long silence over the phone line. "Honey, how do you accidentally marry someone? And who was the accidental groom?"

"Oh, Mom, it was the most wonderful and oddest thing." Chloe went on to explain about the little church, the language difficulties, and how she found herself unknowingly married to Gary.

"You married Gary Erickson? After all that happened between you two, I thought you didn't care for him."

Chloe heard the confusion in her mom's voice. "Things have changed, Mom. I'm not really sure what's going to happen. I'm just glad to be here with him, and I'll enjoy every last moment I have." She lowered her voice in case someone might overhear her conversation. "I'd like to think we can patch things up, but I'm not expecting that. It would be asking too much of either one of us. But it doesn't matter. He's going to have the marriage annulled as soon as we get back to the States."

"If you love him, why can't you make the marriage work?"

Chloe sighed. "Love him? Love isn't an issue. He says he cares, but I'm not sure what to believe. I think it's best I forget the whole thing."

"You don't think he's worth fighting for? Honey, you've never given up anything you wanted."

"Mom, it's easier to stay single. I'd better go. This is an expensive call," she said as Gary walked into the room.

"All right, honey. I'll be praying for you. Don't worry about your father."

"Thanks, Mom. Bye."

Gary's frown deepened. As she hung up the phone he asked, "Is that really how you feel? It's easier to stay single than to invest in another person and allow yourself to be vulnerable?"

Chloe's chin rose fractionally. "Maybe."

Gary's eyes sparkled with determination as he stared at her. "I will not give up so easily. You can't expect me to turn off my feelings as easily as you do. I've made a lot of mistakes that I'll probably regret the rest of my life. I never should have left. But I'm here now. And I'm going to do everything I can to renew that love we lost. Don't you see that we're meant for each other? It's not just my plan but God's. You're my wife, Chloe!"

"Why didn't you come home after the two years were over? You know, when the marine excursion was finished?"

Gary had turned to leave, but Chloe's words stilled him. "I did. Don't you remember? You wrote me that note saying you were happy without me and never wanted to see me again."

Chloe felt like someone had punched her in the stomach. "I never wrote you any note, Gary. I never knew you came home," she whispered.

"But your father said—"

"My father! You believed my father? He always hated you, and he didn't want you hanging around the house. How could you believe him?" She turned her back to him, sickened by the rush of emotion. It didn't matter. Nothing mattered. Even if her father had pushed him away, Gary still chose to leave in the first place. "Please forget about me, Gary. It could never work anyway," she said, looking over her shoulder.

She looked away from the pained expression that passed over Gary's face. He paused in the doorway. "I've never been able to forget about you, Chloe. And I'll never stop loving you."

nine

Chloe sat on the sandy shore of Rancho Nuevo and scanned the ocean waves with the binoculars. She knew Daisy was out there. Somewhere. The tracking system showed the turtle surfacing close to the beach. What was she waiting for? This was the big moment. It was everything this trip had centered around. All Daisy had to do was leave the water, scoot up on the beach, and lay her eggs. Excitement mingled with dread. In one sense, Chloe couldn't wait to see it happen. Gary and the other members of his team had waited a long time for this event. But as soon as it was over and Daisy had taken steps to bring in another generation, the trip would be over. Then she would have no reason to see Gary again.

A frown creased Chloe's brow. She could feel Gary staring at her. There was a tight crackling tension between them that never existed before. Chloe knew she had hurt him, and she didn't know how to make it better. Even Brent and Jennifer noticed the tension and sent Chloe troubled glances. It was probably good the trip was about over.

The sun was up, and the air was hot despite the strong wind that whipped Chloe's hair and clothes. She wished she'd remembered to put her hair up before they had come ashore hours earlier. Gary had wanted to be on the beach before any of the turtles left the water to build nests.

The nesting beach was more acclaimed than Chloe expected. Biologists from all over the world came each year to witness the nesting that took place anytime from April to July. Students from the University of Michoacan of Mexico also helped with the nesting. At the gated entrance, Professor Juan Gonzales met them. He had just finished patrolling the beach on his four-wheel ATV. He was happy to bring Gary and his team up-to-date.

"We've already seen one round of nesting this season, and we have seventy-five nests marked with stakes. We're hoping for the next arribada any time now."

"Arribada?" Chloe asked.

"Yes, it means 'great arrival.' The Kemp's ridleys all leave the water at the same time and nest in unison. It's very exciting to see."

Professor Gonzales led Gary and the others to a place on the beach where they could observe without hindering any of the other biologists. They set up camp and waited.

Chloe swung her binoculars toward the choppy waves. Daisy was swimming in those waves. Along with her, hundreds of turtles would soon come out of the water to nest. Chloe was surprised there were only a few to be seen. She was about to turn away when she spotted a turtle crawling out of the water a few yards away from her. It flapped awkwardly out of the waves and onto the sandy beach.

"Look! Look, look!" she called softly even though she wanted to shout it. She forced herself to move slowly and cautiously back up the beach to where Gary and the others sat. Chloe pointed to the pale-headed turtle, but the others were already fixed on it. "It's so close to us. I wish it were Daisy."

"Look!" Jennifer exclaimed. Three more female turtles lumbered out of the water and up the beach behind the first.

"None of them are Daisy." Using the binoculars, Chloe carefully scanned the expanse of beach as far as she could. "What if she doesn't come? Maybe it was just a natural urge for her to come down to this beach, but she won't lay any eggs."

"She won't come here unless she's going to nest," Gary

answered. He gently pulled the binoculars from her fingers and lifted them to his eyes. He didn't seem to realize Chloe was watching him. He gazed at a far point of the beach where dozens of turtles were coming out of the water and contending for space. The beach stretched for twenty miles, so it was impossible to see all the turtles. But there were many coming from the water at once.

"What if we miss her? It's such a long beach." Chloe flopped down on a beach blanket and kicked hot sand off her feet.

"We'll do our best," Gary answered. "We can fairly accurately pinpoint her location with the tracking device. Right now it looks like she's about thirty feet from shore if my guess is right. I can't say we'll know exactly where she will emerge or what day that will be. But we do know there won't be too many Kemp's ridleys with a tracking device on their shell. We'll keep tracking her with the laptop. I feel pretty confident we'll see her."

"And if we don't?" Chloe persisted.

Gary shrugged. "Then we'll take eggs from one of these other clutches. We have a max of nine days here. If we don't see her, then I have permission from the Mexican government and ours to take some of these eggs back to Texas."

Chloe turned back to the sight on the beach. More turtles were coming out of the water. Some had already found suitable locations and were digging. Sand went flying in all directions as the turtles dug deep holes for their nests.

"They really do come out at the same time," Chloe mused. More turtles came out of the ocean and lumbered up the beach.

"That's why it's called the great arrival. This is the third arribadas I've witnessed. There's nothing like it. Kemp's ridleys are the only sea turtles that have mass nestings. Most sea turtles come out alone, nest alone, then leave by themselves. Kemp's like to take care of it with all their sisters. And they'll nest two or three times in a season." He turned to Chloe with a wide grin on his face. "I love this!" He handed the binoculars back to Chloe.

"Look over there," he pointed. Chloe could feel his excitement. She followed the direction he was pointing. There were five large females paddling through the sand. One of them had a small rectangular tracking device on its shell!

Chloe sucked in her breath. "Is it her?"

"I'm pretty sure. She's the only one with a tracking device. Grab the gear, everyone! We want to get set up before she senses our presence." Brent and Jennifer hurried to do his bidding.

Chloe noticed the vultures circling overhead—predators waiting for the kill. "They won't attack Daisy, will they?" she asked, pointing to the large, watchful birds.

Gary shook his head. "No. The nesting females are too large. Those birds are after the eggs, if they can get them. They'll be back when the little hatchlings make their dash to the water. You can't see them right now, but no doubt there are coyotes pacing the fence, wishing for a chance to get at the eggs, too."

"It's amazing any of them survive without protection. There are land creatures waiting to eat the defenseless turtles before they even hatch. And in the water they have gulls and fish waiting to eat them." Chloe felt a connection to these fascinating creatures unlike anything she had ever experienced. It was amazing to see them go through the different phases in their lives. She wished she could see the hatchlings when they came out of their nests.

"God makes sure enough survive. Now that the poachers aren't allowed here, these little guys have a better chance of making it. Before there were laws protecting sea turtles, they were open prey to ridiculous uses. Now the biggest threat to the turtles is drowning in shrimp nets. Thankfully there is a way fishermen can modify their nets to allow the turtles to escape." As Gary explained these things to Chloe, his gaze was fixed on Daisy.

"Jennifer, hand me the video camera," he ordered. "We need to move closer."

Chloe grabbed all the supplies Gary needed for recording the event: digital and 35mm cameras, notepad for sketching, his laptop, and an extra battery for the video camera.

"Don't we need to hurry? We don't want to miss it," Chloe asked.

Gary's grin stretched across his face. "I keep forgetting you're new to this. Don't worry. It's going to take hours."

After gathering their gear, the four of them made a wide circle around Daisy. Gary chose a location several yards up the beach from where Daisy was already digging. "Now go slow. We're at a disadvantage here since Kemp's nest in the daylight. Don't let her sense your movement. And don't talk! Any noise or movement might alarm her. We want her to nest!"

Chloe and the others sat for over an hour, watching in fascination as Daisy dug out a wide hole for her nest. Sand flew three yards in every direction. Chloe wondered if the turtle had been out of the water for too long. Didn't they dry out and die like fish? No one else seemed concerned so Chloe assumed this was natural turtle behavior, even though the whole nesting process seemed highly unusual.

Next Daisy scooped out sand in the spot under her short tail, then she stopped and rested.

"She's tired," Gary whispered in Chloe's ear. Chloe stiffened. She didn't realize he was so close to her. A shiver ran down her neck where his breath tickled her. "Watch this part," he whispered again.

Daisy raised her head, her tail pointed down, and slowly eggs began dropping into the hole she'd dug. They were about the size of Ping-Pong balls. Over the next hour they watched the turtle lay around one hundred eggs. The hole was filled, and the job was almost finished. After resting a second time, Daisy pulled sand over her nest, using her flippers, and covered the eggs she had laid.

"She's almost finished," Gary commented softly. "Now she'll remove any traces of the nest so no predators can find the eggs, and she'll slip back into the water. She'll probably come back to nest again. Too bad we won't be here to see it."

Chloe watched in amazement as Daisy did exactly as Gary predicted. Once the nest was properly concealed, the turtle made its awkward trek back to the waves and slid into the ocean.

"Mark that at two hours and fifty-five minutes," Gary ordered Brent. His voice was no longer gentle now that Daisy was back in the water.

Chloe glanced at her watch in surprise. Almost three hours had passed. The time seemed to fly by as she watched Daisy make her nest. It was fascinating, and she wanted to see it again and again. It amazed her how God had made these wonderful creatures. They nested in one part of the ocean, grew up in another, then bred in a completely different place. How did they know where to return? How did Daisy know how to build her first nest? God's hand was evident in everything she saw.

"Let's get these eggs in the padded casing and get them back to the boat," Gary barked.

Jennifer and Brent jumped to do his bidding while Chloe hung back and watched them. They worked quickly, carefully digging up the fresh eggs and depositing them gently into the plush boxes.

Chloe moved closer out of curiosity. "What do they feel like?" she asked as she watched Gary carefully handle a tiny egg.

He turned and handed it to her. Chloe took the egg, surprised by how it felt. It wasn't hard like she expected. Instead, it felt soft and rubbery and slippery.

"It's amazing how small the egg is," she marveled. A tiny turtle was growing inside. When it hatched out of the soft shell it would only be about one and one-half inches long! And if the hatchling survived, it would grow into a hundred-pound turtle.

"We'll take these to the boat, Professor Gary," Brent announced. Both he and Jennifer held a box containing the precious eggs.

Gary nodded. "Great. That will give me a chance to jot down a few more observations here and talk to Professor Gonzales. I want to get those eggs secure as quickly as possible."

Chloe trailed Brent and Jennifer at a distance. She noticed they seemed to be arguing. She closed quickly on them, not wanting to eavesdrop but unable to avoid doing so. Brent and Jennifer seemed to forget that they were on the way to the boat and apparently had no idea that Chloe could hear them.

"You can't do it, Brent. It's too dangerous."

Chloe stiffened, stopping in her tracks.

"They're worth a fortune. There are still some Mexicans who think these eggs are an aphrodisiac. One sale will cover me for a while. I'll make the exchange with my contact tonight."

Jennifer shook her head. "I can't do this! It's wrong, and you know it, Brent! I won't—"

"Jennifer!" Brent set the box down on the sand, and Chloe cringed at his rough handling. She was glad Gary hadn't seen it. He would be furious!

Brent drew Jennifer toward him and tipped her face up so he could plant a kiss on her lips. Jennifer's frown instantly vanished to be replaced with a blissful smile. "You know I'm only doing this for us, Jennifer. You want me happy, don't you? What's a few eggs when there are thousands on the beach? They'll never miss a dozen or so."

Jennifer nodded, her eyes shining with admiration. "You really love me?" she asked.

Brent nodded. "You know I do, and that's why I know you'll help me, because of our love for each other."

Chloe wanted to throw up. Brent was lying, and she knew it. Why couldn't Jennifer see the truth? Brent didn't love her! He was manipulating the poor girl's emotions so she would serve him. Chloe realized she had to do something. Brent was about to do something illegal, and he was going to involve Jennifer. Once Brent and Jennifer were a safe distance away, Chloe turned and rushed back to Gary.

"Gary, Brent's going to sell the eggs!"

Frowning, Gary looked up from the notes he was concentrating on. "What? What are you saying?"

"I said Brent's planning to sell the eggs."

"I don't think so, Chloe," he said simply and went back to his notes.

Chloe stared at him in amazement. He didn't react. No emotion. No response.

"You don't believe me? I overheard them. Brent told Jennifer he's planning to sell the eggs."

Gary let out a long-suffering sigh. "Brent's brazen, but he's not stupid. It's risky business selling turtle eggs. He wouldn't know who to sell them to even if he had the notion to make some money."

"But, Gary! I heard them talking! You said yourself you

thought someone was involved with poachers. He's planning to sell them to his contact tonight!"

Gary shook his head. "There's no one around here that would dare take them off his hands. Look at this place! Fences, people patrolling—the government protects turtle eggs. Anyone caught with them would be in hot water. Brent might think he can sell them, but no one is going to take them. Our eggs are safe."

Chloe wished she shared his optimism.

❧

Back on The Bounty Chloe found Uncle Howard fishing off the aft deck. "How's the nesting going?" he asked as Chloe, Gary, Jennifer, and Brent stepped on board.

"Great!" Gary answered. "Daisy already nested, and we have a full clutch of eggs to take back to the States. We've had a profitable day. How about you?" he asked, indicating the fishing.

Uncle Howard shrugged. "It's a little warm, and the fish aren't biting, but any day of fishing is a good day."

As the others went into the salon, Chloe lingered by her uncle. She watched him make a perfect cast then tighten the line.

"What's on your mind, Chloe-girl?"

"Uncle Howard, Brent and Jennifer are involved with poachers. They are going to steal the eggs, and Professor Gary doesn't believe me. Is there anything you can do?"

Howard shrugged. "I just provide the transportation. I'm not responsible for what happens to the client's cargo. If Brent steals the eggs, and Gary doesn't do anything about it, it's not my problem."

Chloe was dumbfounded by her uncle's disinterest. "How can you say that? Don't you care that this endangered species is going to be harmed? Doesn't it bother you to know that Brent is involved in something illegal? They're dealing with poachers!"

Howard reeled in his line. "You've done what you can do. You brought your suspicions before Gary, and he didn't do anything about it. Leave it alone. It's his problem now."

Chloe shook her head. She couldn't understand her uncle's careless attitude. "I can't leave it like this! I care too much about those helpless sea creatures."

Howard gave his niece a thoughtful look. "Are you sure it's the turtles you care so much about? Or is it the professor?"

Chloe felt the warmth flow into her cheeks. "My feelings for Gary have nothing to do with this situation!" she snapped.

Howard chuckled at Chloe's indignation. "And I can't believe you protest so strongly. You fuss about turtle eggs, but I think there's more to this story. You've been fighting your feelings for a long time. Maybe it's time to let go and give love a second chance."

Chloe grimaced at her uncle. "You aren't going to help me save the turtle eggs?"

Uncle Howard rebaited his hook and cast out the line again. "Chloe, it's not my problem. Don't try to make it your problem, either."

❧

Later that evening everyone was relaxed and celebrating the successful mission. Even Uncle Howard joined in the merriment.

"Our Daisy is the best turtle!" Brent said. "She could have waited to come out and nest on the last day, but she chose the first. She's a good girl." Chloe frowned when he gave her a flirtatious wink. He professed his love for Jennifer then flirted with Chloe. She returned his wink with a scowl.

"I'm so glad we didn't have to sit on the beach for a week, waiting for her," Jennifer added.

"It's amazing how many eggs will be laid on that one beach," Chloe mused.

"Yeah, imagine the cash flow we'd have. It's a gold mine that can't be touched," Brent muttered.

Chloe stared at him in consternation. She knew what he was up to. Hadn't Gary or her uncle heard Brent's comment? Was she the only one who suspected him or even cared? How could Jennifer go along with his deceptions?

Brent rose then drew Jennifer to her feet. "We're going into town to celebrate. There's a little shop with handcrafted jewelry that I told Jennifer I would take her to before we left. I'm sure no one else wants to come along."

"I hope it isn't like the last shop Jennifer and I went to," Chloe said with meaning. Jennifer looked away with discomfort. Chloe wanted to shake the girl and tell her to come to her senses. "I should go along. I'm supposed to chaperone Jennifer."

Chloe stood to her feet, but Brent shook his head. "No, no! Don't trouble yourself. We're just going to do a little shopping. Nothing to worry about." He slipped his arm around Jennifer's shoulders. "I'll take good care of her."

Chloe frowned at the familiar contact. She knew it was a farce. Brent didn't really care about Jennifer. She wished the girl could see what was going on.

But what did it matter? Jennifer believed Brent loved her. Gary didn't believe the eggs were in danger. And Uncle Howard didn't want any involvement. Chloe turned away and headed toward her stateroom. There was nothing she could do. Her only hope was that God would expose Brent before any damage was done.

Gary didn't look up from the notepad in his lap. "Don't worry about them, Chloe. They'll be fine. Stay on board and relax if you don't feel like going into town. I'm working on my notes. You can do what you want. Maybe we could talk," he added with meaning.

"Hold up, you two," Uncle Howard called to Brent and Jennifer. "I don't want you taking the dinghy out at night. I'll take you over."

Brent didn't look pleased, but he didn't argue either. "All right. Let's go."

≈

The talk between Chloe and Gary never took place. He was too concerned with his notes after the nesting. It was just as well. Chloe wasn't ready to discuss anything with him until she had a chance to sort through her feelings. At the moment they were a jumbled mess, and she didn't want to deal with them.

She was just about asleep when she heard voices up on deck. She changed into her shorts and an oversized T-shirt and crept upstairs to investigate. She hoped it was just Brent and Jennifer returning, but her gut instinct told her it was something else.

A high-speed boat was pulled up next to The Bounty. Bright spotlights were pointed at the deck. Two Mexican officers were talking with Gary and by the deep scowl on his face, something was wrong.

"We have reasons to suspect you for poaching, Señor Erickson," one of the officers said.

"What reasons? I'm not a poacher!"

"Please come with us, Señor, so we can discuss this at the police station."

Gary ran his hand through his already mussed hair. "This

is ludicrous. If you had any idea what I stand for you would realize how ridiculous these allegations are! I'm not a poacher! I have documentation proving that I'm not a poacher."

"Do you have sea turtle eggs in your possession, Señor?" one of the officers questioned.

"Yes! I have the permission papers from the Mexican government."

"Show me the papers."

Gary turned back to the salon to retrieve the documents. Without speaking, Chloe located the papers he sought and handed them to Gary. He took them with a grim nod of appreciation.

The senior officer read the documents. "It says here you have permission to take up to one hundred eggs back to Texas."

"Yes, that's what I've been trying to tell you! And I have documentation proving that we've taken ninety-six eggs."

"Show me the eggs."

With a sigh of frustration, Gary led the officers into the salon. The officers trailed him cautiously as though they were staking out a possible drug bust. Chloe followed them, making herself available to answer any questions and speed their visit along. So far they didn't even seem to realize she was there.

"Open the box," the officer ordered when Gary pointed to the insulated box that contained the turtle eggs.

With a stiff nod of assent Gary lifted the lid. His gasp of disbelief drew Chloe to his side. She peered into the box, expecting to see dozens of the tiny eggs. Instead, the box was empty.

"You will come with us for questioning," one of the officers said, pointing to Gary.

"You're arresting me? On what grounds are you arresting me?" Gary demanded.

"We have reason to believe you have sold the eggs illegally. We protect the turtles and must prosecute anyone who harms the species."

A muscle worked in Gary's jaw. "Get your uncle, Chloe," he murmured. "I could use his help."

"He isn't here. He took Brent and Jennifer to town. They aren't back yet," she reminded helplessly.

"He's gone, and the eggs are gone," Gary repeated. Chloe could read the accusation in his gaze.

"He didn't do it, Gary! Uncle Howard wouldn't steal the eggs. It was Brent—and Jennifer helped him."

"You don't know that for sure, Chloe."

"I do. I do know! I tried to tell you this afternoon!"

Gary shook his head. "We have to figure this out. I'm in serious trouble here." Reluctantly he followed the officers onto the speedboat. The docking ropes were drawn in, and the boat sped away into the darkness.

Chloe looked around helplessly. The eggs were gone. Gary had been arrested. And her uncle wasn't there to help. "Please, Lord, show me what to do!" She sagged down on a deck chair with a sigh. Who knew what would happen in the Mexican jail? She had heard horror stories of foreigners being locked away and forgotten. Minutes ticked by into an hour as Chloe waited.

She had plenty of time to consider her relationship with Gary. Since their impromptu wedding he had worked hard to convince her she needed to forgive him. She didn't believe it was an issue of forgiveness, but rather an issue of self-preservation. She never wanted to hurt like that again. But, she reasoned, if she didn't take a chance, she would never experience love like that again, either. And she wanted that love! She still loved Gary—with all that was humanly possible. She loved him. It was hard to admit, yet it felt right. It was as though a hard knot had been released from her chest, and she was free. God had healed her heart! God had taken her heart of stone and had given her a heart of flesh. She didn't know when it happened. She no longer wanted to hold back. She was still afraid, but the fear no longer paralyzed her. Gary was her husband, and she loved him.

In the distance she heard a motorboat. It wasn't as loud as the high-speed boat the police came in. Chloe peered into the darkness, hoping she could see who might be coming. It was her uncle! But he was alone.

"Oh, Uncle Howard! Gary's in trouble. . . ." Chloe paused, staring at the empty seats. "Where are Brent and Jennifer?" she asked as he pulled close to The Bounty.

"They're still in town—"

"We have to go back! Gary's been taken to jail—the eggs are missing! I just know Brent did it, but Gary wouldn't listen—"

"Stop gabbing, girl, and get in the boat. I've come back to get you."

Chloe hopped into the inflated boat, and they sped toward the shore. The dinghy skimmed quickly over the water, but it seemed to take an eternity. Finally they reached a pier where they could dock. "Quick, Uncle Howard, we have to get Gary!"

"Why do you care what happens to him, Chloe? Is it because he's your boss?" her uncle asked as he tied off the little boat.

"No!" Chloe exclaimed absently as she scrambled onto the dock. "It's because I love him!" She halted at the sudden admission and stared in bewilderment at her uncle. "You knew, didn't you?"

Howard chuckled. His belly shook with merriment. "Of course. It's been written across your face for the last few weeks. I knew it was just a matter of time before you admitted it for yourself."

"I think I've known for a while, but I didn't want to face it. And now that I've faced it, I'm scared to get hurt again. What if he leaves me like he did before?"

Uncle Howard patted Chloe's shoulder. "Let love have its perfect course. In the meantime, we need to get your professor out of jail!"

❧

"How do you know where to go?" Chloe asked as she followed her uncle down the darkened streets.

"I've been here a time or two," Howard answered. He walked up to a small building and opened the door. He allowed Chloe to pass inside.

Chloe stepped into the small jail, expecting it to be a filthy place of torture. One glance around the tidy office told her she had watched too many movies. She and Howard approached the front desk where a young man in a crisp uniform sat.

"I must see Gary Erickson! Can you take me to him?" She knew she sounded breathless and desperate, but she didn't care. She had to rescue Gary and tell him she still loved him!

"I'm sorry, Señorita. That's impossible at this time," the young officer answered.

Anxiety coiled in the pit of Chloe's stomach. They weren't going to let her see him. What could she do? Somehow she had to convince them he was innocent. She would have to get a lawyer if they wouldn't cooperate. How would she ever do that in this country?

"Please! You must understand. He's innocent! He would

never steal and sell turtle eggs. He's given his life to the study of those creatures. You have to see he wouldn't harm them! Let me see him," she pleaded. "I have to know he's all right."

The officer shook his head. "I'm sorry, Señorita."

Howard put his hand on Chloe's arm. "Let me handle this." He spoke in rapid Spanish to the young officer.

The officer nodded apologetically. "Sí, perdón! I will take you to him, Señora Erickson. Please follow me."

Chloe gave her uncle a curious look but didn't say anything. Señora Erickson? Uncle Howard smiled mischievously as they followed the officer down the hall. Chloe expected him to lead them to the jail cells housing prisoners. Instead he stopped beside an office door. He pushed the door open and allowed Chloe and Howard to step inside the room. She found Gary and Jennifer sitting across a table from an officer. Confused, Chloe looked from one person to another.

"Who is this?" the senior officer asked.

"Señora Erickson. Ella está aquí para estar con su marido," the young officer said, bowing his way out the door.

"What's going on?" Chloe demanded. She'd expected to find Gary behind bars, but he was calmly having a cup of coffee with the local law enforcement. And where was Brent?

The younger officer motioned to one of the chairs, so Chloe took a seat, perching on the edge of it.

"Tell me your name," the senior officer insisted.

"Chloe Crenshaw," she answered. "Where is Brent? Has something happened?" She glanced around the table, but no one offered any answers. Her uncle sat back in his chair with his arms crossed over his chest. Jennifer was clearly upset and stared down at her clasped hands. Gary returned her gaze, but didn't say anything.

"My aide introduced you as Señora Erickson. You say

Crenshaw. What is right?"

The officer tapped his pencil against the table, waiting for her answer. Chloe felt the heat rise to her cheeks, and she knew everyone was staring at her. "I—we—that is. . ." She looked helplessly at Gary.

Gary pulled a document from his pocket Chloe recognized as their marriage certificate. "Here, maybe this will clear things up." He slid the paper across the table to the officer.

The officer quickly read over the certificate. "This is your marriage certificate? From Shepherd's Fold Christian Church in Punta de Piedra?"

Both Chloe and Gary nodded.

The officer smiled widely. "Then you aren't truly married. The church certificate is not legal. You must also have a legal license signed by a Mexican judge."

"We're not really married?" Chloe asked.

"No, Señorita. You are not really married to Señor Erickson without the state's approval. There are many documents besides the church's certificate."

Feeling like her world tilted wildly, Chloe demanded, "Would someone please tell me what's going on here?" Tears stung her eyes as she stared at Gary. He wordlessly stared back.

"I think I should be the one to explain," Howard said. He stood and began pacing the small area behind the table. "While I don't care as much about the turtles as some people, I realized I had to take some responsibility as far as young Brent was concerned. Chloe knew Brent was up to no good, and he even tried to get Jennifer involved. The men he was working for wouldn't care if Brent lived or not, so I knew I had to stop him." He paused, giving Jennifer a sympathetic look. Tears filled the young girl's eyes.

"I never should have believed him!" she wailed as she dabbed her eyes with a tissue.

Howard continued. "I followed the two of them. Brent was carrying a backpack, and I suspected it held the turtle eggs. They went to a shop on the edge of town, and Brent disappeared inside. Jennifer had sense enough to stay outside."

"I've been in one of those places before. I never wanted to go back." Jennifer shivered.

"I figured Brent was making the exchange, so I grabbed Jennifer and convinced her to go with me to the policia."

"I thank God you showed up when you did. They were about to throw me in a prison cell with some tough-looking men," Gary added. He turned to Chloe. "If your uncle hadn't arrived and explained everything, I'd still be in trouble. I never should have doubted you or him."

"It's water under the bridge, Professor," Howard said, accepting the apology. "The police went to the shop to apprehend Brent and the poachers before any of them could get away. They retrieved the stolen turtle eggs, unharmed, and also impounded a lot of illegal drugs."

"So now what happens?" Chloe asked, turning to the senior officer.

"You're all free to go."

"And Brent? What about him?" she asked, turning to Gary.

"He has to stay." There was no further explanation, and Chloe didn't press it. All she wanted was to get back to The Bounty and put this terrible evening behind her.

The four of them left the police station and headed toward the pier where the dinghy was docked. The ride back to The Bounty was quiet. It seemed strange without Brent. Chloe put a comforting arm around Jennifer and murmured, "He never valued the real treasure in you."

Jennifer nodded and sniffed. "I know. And I don't think I'll ever be such a fool again. You were right—it's easier to stay single."

Chloe looked across the boat at Gary, the man she loved. "No, Jennifer. I'd give all I have to be with the man I love. It may be easier to stay single, but love is worth the risk."

&

Chloe was stepping across the threshold into her stateroom when she heard her name.

"Chloe, can I talk to you?" Gary stepped near. "Not here, though. Let's go up to the flybridge where we won't be interrupted."

Chloe followed him up to the top deck, wondering what he wanted to talk to her about. Had he changed his mind about her? Maybe he'd decided loving her wasn't worth the effort. Fear pricked her heart, but she quickly pressed it away. She would face whatever he had to say—God would give her strength to deal with it.

Up on the flybridge a warm breeze teased Chloe's hair. The stars were twinkling brightly overhead and in the distance she could see the town's lights. It was a lovely evening. Gary motioned Chloe to the softly padded bench.

Chloe peered at him through the darkness. She couldn't make out his blue eyes or the expression on his face, but she knew he was staring back at her.

"I wanted to talk to you about our marriage," he said, taking out the certificate. He gently smoothed out the creases.

"Are you relieved it wasn't legitimate? Now we don't have to get it annulled." A stab of disappointment shot through her. Somehow she would deal with losing him again if he wanted to go.

"Why would I be relieved? Haven't you listened to a word

I've said, Chloe? I never intended to get it annulled. I've been trying to convince you that I love you and we should stay married."

"What about the past? We can't just erase all that happened. While I suffered for six years, you never gave me a second thought."

"I never stopped thinking about you. I'm always thinking about you," Gary answered softly. He knelt before Chloe, taking her hands in his gentle grasp. "Do you honestly believe you're the only one who suffered? I spent two years longing for you, only to find you had moved on. How could I know your father had lied to me? I spent the next years wishing for something I thought would never be. Imagine what I suffered when I read about your engagement in the paper! I knew I deserved the pain, but that didn't make it easier to bear. I took the job at the university hoping for a chance to be near you again. Don't you see God has given us a second chance? I'm asking you for one more beginning. I love you, Chloe. Will you marry me? I want you to be my wife—for keeps."

Chloe sucked in her breath. He wanted her. There was no reason to fear. There was no more room for doubt. For keeps. "Loving you is all I've ever wanted to do," she whispered. He was the man God had chosen to be her husband. She knew that with all her heart.

"You'll marry me?"

"Yes!"

Gary kissed her with barely contained joy. After a moment he pulled away. "I have an idea, and it's a crazy idea." He paused, and Chloe nodded for him to continue. "What would you say about going back to the police station tomorrow and making our marriage legal? We already have the blessing of the church. All this time we thought we were married."

Chloe followed his train of thought. "I already told my mom that we're married. It may be a little awkward to say it was all a misunderstanding and then get married again."

"We could have a reception for friends and family as soon as we get back home."

"And you would be with me to face my father," Chloe said with a sigh of relief.

Gary drew her closer to him. "I'll be with you for the rest of our lives."

ten

It's going to be fine," Gary said as he laced his fingers with Chloe's. He handled the steering wheel with his free hand, maneuvering the quiet neighborhood streets.

Chloe gave him a tentative smile. She suddenly felt shy. The past four days had been wonderful.

She and Gary had gotten married through the local Mexican judge. The judge, thankfully bilingual, had been understanding of their unusual situation. Conscious of time, he had taken extra steps to see that all documentation was filled out and filed quickly. He then performed a brief ceremony, in English, on the beach. It couldn't have been more beautiful. There were still a dozen turtles paddling up the beach. Jennifer served as Chloe's maid of honor, and Uncle Howard was Gary's best man. Chloe wore a beautiful flowered sundress and had a wreath of fresh flowers in her hair. Gary, on the other hand, wore his best khaki shorts and a Hawaiian shirt. They were both barefoot in the sand with the ocean waves crashing behind him. It was the ceremony Chloe had always dreamed of.

Unfortunately Brent hadn't been able to witness the ceremony. He was being held in prison for poaching turtle eggs until he could secure a good lawyer. "Brent's going to be all right, isn't he?" Chloe asked, seeking reassurance.

"He's going to be fine. He won't have it easy, but it's a better way than the path he was on. If your uncle hadn't stopped him, Brent might have gotten involved with drug trafficking or smuggling. Or he might have been killed. This way Brent will have the chance to turn his life around. He has so much potential."

Chloe patted Gary's hand. "Hopefully he'll make good choices now. I'm glad Uncle Howard was there to save the turtle eggs. It will be exciting to see the hatchlings dig their way out of the Texas beach in a few months."

"They'll be really tiny, about the size of a half dollar. You'll love them. They paddle their way as fast as they can down the beach and into the waves."

"Maybe Uncle Howard will be back in time. He'll love seeing that. He seemed reluctant to leave us in Tampico when he had to take his next job."

Uncle Howard had taken them, including Jennifer, from Rancho Nuevo to Tampico. There he loaded the boat with fresh supplies, and the new clients boarded. Rather than taking on a turtle observation crew, he was escorting wealthy passengers on a leisure tour down to Belize. He said the round-trip would take him a few months.

Jennifer also left Gary and Chloe in Tampico. They dropped her off at the airport, and she bade them a teary farewell. Chloe tried to remind her that God had a special man for her that would recognize her preciousness. Jennifer seemed discouraged and guilt-ridden over the happenings with Brent. Gary made her understand that she was forgiven. He looked forward to her joining another expedition—they might track some of Daisy's hatchlings. After Jennifer was safely on board the plane, Chloe and Gary were left alone to enjoy four days of honeymooning in Tampico.

"It was quite an adventure, wasn't it?" Chloe said, staring at Gary's profile. He squeezed her hand in agreement, a smile bringing light to his eyes. Chloe sighed in contentment, feeling as though she was dreaming. She was truly Mrs. Gar

Erickson. After so much difficulty they had found their way back to each other. God had made it possible for her to experience the love she thought was lost forever. They had discovered the real treasure within each other.

"We're here, sweetheart," Gary said, pulling Chloe out of her reverie. He had pulled his car into the driveway of her parents' home. Chloe's heart rate suddenly rose with the thought of facing her father. He would be furious. She had gone off on an excursion that was foolish in his eyes. When Trevor came to retrieve her in Mexico, she hadn't come home with him. And then she got married! What would her father say? She hoped he wouldn't overreact and cause himself more health problems. *Please, Lord, let Dad understand. For once, let him be happy for me.*

Peace beyond all understanding flooded Chloe's heart. She wanted her dad's approval, yet she knew she could be happy with or without his consent. Above all, she knew she had the Lord's blessing. Nothing was more important. God had given her a husband who was gentle and kind—one who had always delighted in her.

"It'll be all right. Trust me," Gary said reassuringly, taking ahold of her hand. He pressed a kiss to her cheek.

Chloe beamed at him. "I know it will."

Together they approached the front door and knocked. Only a few seconds passed before the door was thrown open and her father stood in the doorway, staring at them.

Chloe took a deep, steadying breath. "Dad, you remember Gary Erickson. He's my husband."

Seconds passed into what seemed like minutes as Chloe waited for her dad to respond. She expected him to explode, rage incoherently, then slam the door in her face. Slowly the frown lifted off his forehead and a slight smile tugged at the corners of his mouth. "Allison," he hollered over his shoulder, "come greet our new son-in-law!"

Astonished, Chloe glanced at Gary. The look he gave her melted her heart. It was going to be all right, just as he promised.

A Letter To Our Readers

Dear Reader:

In order that we might better contribute to your reading enjoyment, we would appreciate your taking a few minutes to respond to the following questions. We welcome your comments and read each form and letter we receive. When completed, please return to the following:

Fiction Editor
Heartsong Presents
PO Box 719
Uhrichsville, Ohio 44683

1. Did you enjoy reading *Real Treasure* by Tish Davis?
   ❏ Very much! I would like to see more books by this author!
   ❏ Moderately. I would have enjoyed it more if

   _____

   _____

   _____

2. Are you a member of **Heartsong Presents**?   ❏ Yes   ❏ No
   If no, where did you purchase this book? _____

   _____

3. How would you rate, on a scale from 1 (poor) to 5 (superior), the cover design? _____

4. On a scale from 1 (poor) to 10 (superior), please rate the following elements.

   ____ Heroine   ____ Plot
   ____ Hero   ____ Inspirational theme
   ____ Setting   ____ Secondary characters

5. These characters were special because? _____

_____

_____

6. How has this book inspired your life? _____

_____

_____

7. What settings would you like to see covered in future **Heartsong Presents** books? _____

_____

_____

8. What are some inspirational themes you would like to see treated in future books? _____

_____

_____

9. Would you be interested in reading other **Heartsong Presents** titles? ❏ Yes   ❏ No

10. Please check your age range:

   ❏ Under 18   ❏ 18-24
   ❏ 25-34   ❏ 35-45
   ❏ 46-55   ❏ Over 55

Name _____

Occupation _____

Address _____

SAN FRANCISCO

4 stories in 1

Four independent women in the San Francisco bay area are about to be swept into a wave of romance.

Letting go to romance will take each woman a step of new faith. Will the arms of love catch them— or will they be shattered by a dream?

Four complete inspirational romance stories by author Kristin Billerbeck.

Contemporary, paperback, 464 pages, 5 $^3/_{16}$" x 8"

_____

Hearts♥ng

Any 12
Heartsong
Presents titles
for only
$27.00*

CONTEMPORARY ROMANCE IS CHEAPER BY THE DOZEN!

Buy any assortment of twelve *Heartsong Presents* titles and save 25% off of the already discounted price of $2.97 each!

*plus $2.00 shipping and handling per order and sales tax where applicable.

HEARTSONG PRESENTS TITLES AVAILABLE NOW:

(If ordering from this page, please remember to include it with the order form.)

Presents

Great Inspirational Romance at a Great Price!

Heartsong Presents books are inspirational romances in contemporary and historical settings, designed to give you an enjoyable, spirit-lifting reading experience. You can choose wonderfully written titles from some of today's best authors like Hannah Alexander, Andrea Boeshaar, Yvonne Lehman, Tracie Peterson, and many others.

When ordering quantities less than twelve, above titles are $2.97 each.
Not all titles may be available at time of order.

HEARTSONG
PRESENTS

If you love Christian romance...

$10.⁹⁹

You'll love Heartsong Presents' inspiring and faith-filled romances by today's very best Christian authors...DiAnn Mills, Wanda E. Brunstetter, and Yvonne Lehman, to mention a few!

When you join Heartsong Presents, you'll enjoy 4 brand-new mass market, 176–page books—two contemporary and two historical—that will build you up in your faith when you discover God's role in every relationship you read about!

Imagine...four new romances every four weeks—with men and women like you who long to meet the one God has chosen as the love of their lives...all for the low price of $10.99 postpaid.

To join, simply visit www.heartsong presents.com or complete the coupon below and mail it to the address provided.

Mass Market 176 Page

YES! Sign me up for Heartsong!